WAITING FOR THE ATTACK

"Where is it, Pa?" Zach whispered. He tried to keep his voice steady so his father wouldn't suspect how scared he felt.

"It could be anywhere. Keep your eyes peeled."

Nate's horse had raised his head to sniff the breeze. Nate could guess why. "Get set," he said softly. "If it's going to attack, it won't wait long."

Zach, struck dumb by terror, made no reply, and he saw his father glance at him. At the very same instant he saw something else: the panther, its claws extended, vaulting from concealment straight at him.

The *Wilderness* series:

#14

WILDERNESS

TENDERFOOT

David Thompson

LEISURE BOOKS   NEW YORK CITY

A LEISURE BOOK®

June 2004

Published by

Dorchester Publishing Co., Inc.
200 Madison Avenue
New York, NY 10016

ISBN 0-8439-3422-0

The name "Leisure Books" and the stylized "L" with design are trademarks of Dorchester Publishing Co., Inc.

Printed in the United States of America.

Visit us on the web at www.dorchesterpub.com.

#14

WILDERNESS

TENDERFOOT

To Judy, Joshua, and Shane.

Prologue

The five Gros Ventres were far from their home range. They had traveled high into the rugged, majestic mountains to the south of their customary haunts, and were strung out in single file as they crested a sloping ridge.

In the lead rode a tall warrior, who now drew rein to scour the verdant land below. Rolling Thunder was his name. He could boast of having counted over 20 coup, and many of his people were of the opinion that when their aged chief died he would be the successor. A born leader, he had led over a dozen successful war parties and never lost a man.

But today Rolling Thunder was not on a raid into enemy territory. His small band was after elk, which thrived in the high mountain valleys where abundant grass and pristine springs, lakes, and streams made the Rockies an animal paradise. So far the elk had been elusive, but he hoped to find some soon.

"Is it wise to keep going south?" a gruff voice asked

behind him. "We are close to Shoshone country."

Rolling Thunder twisted, regarded the speaker for a moment, then grinned. "Are you turning into an old woman, Little Dog? Are you afraid of the Shoshones?"

Before Little Dog could answer, the third warrior in line snorted in contempt and declared, "Only a fool would fear them! Shoshones are all cowards at heart. They run and hide at the sight of real warriors."

Rolling Thunder saw Little Dog's features cloud and spoke to forestall an argument. "I was joking, Loud Talker. All of us know how brave Little Dog is. Was he not the one who saved you from the Dakotas that time they shot your horse out from under you?"

Loud Talker frowned. He had spoken, as usual, without thinking, and as usual, he had upset one of his closest friends. "I did not mean to insult Little Dog," he said. "Yes, he did save me from the Dakotas that time. If not for him my hair would now be hanging in a Dakota lodge."

The last two men joined them. One, a husky warrior named Walking Bear, leaned forward and commented, "We are all brave. But we are few and the Shoshones are many. If a large war party should find us, we would be in for the fight of our lives."

"Good," said the last man, known simply as Bobcat. "We will give our people something to remember us by."

No one responded for several seconds. They all knew Bobcat was too bloodthirsty for his own good, but he was otherwise thoroughly dependable and the best man with a bow in their entire tribe. Bobcat had never lost an archery contest. No matter the distance, he always hit his targets dead center.

Little Dog cleared his throat. "I love a fight as much as any of you, but I see no reason why we should needlessly throw our lives away. If we are all slain, who will take word to our people? How will they learn our fate?" He gestured southward. "The Shoshones are not the cowards Loud Talker claims they are. He has not fought them, as I have done, or he would know they are as fierce as the Blackfeet when aroused."

No one disputed the point. Rolling Thunder noted the unease in some of their eyes and said quickly, "There is no cause for worry. We came here to hunt, not to make war. Our wives need meat to dry and put aside before the cold comes and the snow begins to fall." He straightened and stretched. "So we will avoid the Shoshones if at all possible, not because we are afraid of them but because our families are depending on us."

His words had the desired effect. The others smiled or voiced agreement and Little Dog visibly relaxed.

Pleased with himself, Rolling Thunder rode on. Since he was the organizer of the hunt, it was his responsibility to see that everything went smoothly. If they took to bickering among themselves, they would hunt poorly. They might fail to down a single elk. And under no circumstances would he return to the village empty-handed. Those few who resented his standing in the tribe would whisper behind his back, perhaps spread a rumor that his medicine was gone.

Rolling Thunder would let nothing tarnish his name. He took great pride in his accomplishments. At the age of 15 he had counted his first coup on a Nez Percé, and ever since he had steadily added to his prestige, until he was now widely respected and admired. The old chief came to him regularly for advice. Seats of honor were his at the council sessions. He owned more horses than anyone else, and the beauty of his wives made him the envy of every man. After working so hard to get where he was, he would do whatever was needed to maintain his standing.

Of equal importance in his decision to press on was

the fact he always kept his word. He had promised his wives he would bring them elk meat, and he would not let them down. To his way of thinking a man was no man at all if he could not provide for his loved ones, and he had a reputation for being an excellent provider.

In order to guarantee success, Rolling Thunder had brought his friends to this region where the elk were known to be more numerous than practically anywhere else. It mattered little to him that the Shoshones also hunted here. His wits and his strength had seen him through more dangers than he cared to remember, and he was completely confident he would prevail if he encountered them.

Once in the valley, Rolling Thunder stopped. "We must separate and search for sign. Little Dog and I will take the west side."

"Stay alert," Walking Bear advised, hefting his lance. He angled to the east, Bobcat and Loud Talker tagging along. "We will call out if we find anything."

The only sounds were the dull thud of hoofs and the noisy gurgling of a swift stream meandering along the valley floor. Rolling Thunder's keen dark eyes roved constantly over the ground. A skilled tracker, he sought evidence of a game trail. Where there was water, there was always wildlife. From past experience he knew that any elk in the vicinity would bed down in the dense timber above during the day and come down to drink toward sunset. Being creatures of habit, the elk would use the same route again and again, so if he could find the trail he could backtrack to where they were hiding.

The morning sun climbed higher and higher. They were halfway along the valley when Little Dog addressed him.

"Do you think any of the others suspect the true reason you insisted we come so far south?"

Rolling Thunder's iron will served him in good stead.

He continued riding, his face impassive, and remarked absently, "I do not know what you mean."

"You can fool them, my friend, but not me. We have been like brothers since childhood. I know your ways better than I know my own."

"You speak in riddles."

"Do I?" Little Dog said. "If so, it is a riddle you understand. And I am surprised you have not told them the truth. They are almost as close to you as I am."

"Speak with a straight tongue."

"Very well. Does White Buffalo know what you are up to?"

"Why should I tell him?" Rolling Thunder rejoined, the indignation in his tone obvious. "What is he to me? We are not even related." He was about to go on, to justify himself, when he saw where the grass ahead had been flattened and torn up by the passage of many heavy forms. And there in the bare earth were scores of large elk tracks. "Look!" he exclaimed, then trotted to them.

Rolling Thunder slid down off his war pony and sank to one knee to examine the prints. As his gaze roved along the game trail he suddenly stiffened, then lowered his face within inches of the earth.

"What have you found?" Little Dog asked.

"Fresh horse tracks," Rolling Thunder answered, touching his fingers to one of the depressions. There were two sets of hoofprints, those of a larger than normal animal that must be a big stallion and a much smaller set that might be those of a mare. Both had crossed the valley and gone up into the trees. "Someone else is hunting elk," he deduced, and rose.

"Shoshones, you think?"

"Perhaps," Rolling Thunder said, hiding his disappointment that neither of the animals were shod. Rising, he led his horse toward the stream, studying the tracks carefully as he went along, memorizing the individual characteristics of each animal.

"We will have to stay clear of them," Little Dog said.

"There are only two."

"But there may be many more."

"It will do no harm to follow them and see."

"But what—"

Rolling Thunder spun, anger clouding his expression. "Earlier I stood up for you, but now you give me cause to doubt my judgment. There is a fine line, old friend, between caution and cowardice. See that you do not cross that line or I will denounce you in front of the entire village."

Eyes flinty as steel, Little Dog closed his mouth.

Rolling Thunder spun, and walked on until he came to a spot by the water's edge where the two riders had dismounted and let their animals drink. The moccasin prints told him a large man was riding the stallion, but the rider of the mare was a mere child. If they were alone they would be easy to slay. Rolling Thunder tilted back his head and vented a series of piercing yips in a perfect imitation of a howling coyote.

From the other side of the valley came Walking Bear's prompt reply.

"Maybe we will count coup on this trip after all," Rolling Thunder declared.

Chapter One

"Did you hear something, Pa?"

Nathaniel King turned his amused gazed from an irate, chattering gray squirrel in a nearby pine and shifted in the saddle to stare at his young son. "No, Zach. What was it?"

"I don't rightly know, Pa. Something real faint." The boy had his head cocked and was listening intently. "It came from behind us, I figure."

Nate listened for several seconds, but heard only the temperamental squirrel and the northwesterly wind sighing through the tall trees. He was about to suggest that his inexperienced son had imagined hearing a sound when he saw the earnest look Zachary wore and realized the boy was doing exactly as Nate had often instructed him to do. "Always stay alert in the wilderness," he had repeatedly advised. "The man who stays alive is the man who is never taken by surprise. Use your senses, your eyes and ears and even your

11

nose, like you have never used them before. Use them like the wild beasts do. Learn from the animals, Zach. That's what the Indians have done since the beginning of time."

Nate smiled, pleased that Zach was trying so hard, and said, "If you hear it again, let me know."

"I sure will."

Cradling his heavy Hawken in the crook of his left elbow, Nate lifted the rope reins and clucked his pied gelding into motion. By nightfall or early tomorrow, he reflected, they would have their elk and he would teach Zach the proper way to remove the hide, butcher the carcass, and make jerky. In a week they would be back at the Shoshone village, where he would proudly boast of his son's prowess to all the other fathers.

He had to hand it to his wife. Winona had come up with the idea to take Zach off alone into the high country to hunt. The time had come, she'd asserted, for Zach to learn the all-important skills he would need to survive in the raw, untamed land her tribe called home. Already the boy was a skilled rider and could shoot a bow as well as his Shoshone playmates. But there was so much more Zach needed to know, and no one better qualified to teach him than his own father.

Which tickled Nate no end. He loved being a parent, loved being able to spend the precious time with Zach that his own father had been too busy to spend with him. He delighted in seeing the world through Zach's naive eyes, and in watching Zach slowly grow and mature. In a sense he was reliving his own childhood, and sometimes things that Zach said or did brought back forgotten memories of incidents from his own early years. As Zach discovered more and more of the world, it seemed that Nate rediscovered more and more of himself.

"Say, Pa?"

"Yes?" Nate idly responded as he surveyed the expanse of mountain above. The elk trail they had been following was winding ever higher, and unless he was mistaken he'd find them holed up in a belt of aspens less than a quarter of a mile away. Some of the leaves had begun to change, dotting the green background with patches of bright yellow.

"Why do some of the other boys keep calling me a breed?"

Involuntarily, Nate's grip tightened on the reins and his lips compressed into a thin line. He didn't turn because he was afraid his feelings would show. "Your mother is a Shoshone. I'm a white man. That makes you half-white, half-Indian," he explained. "A half-breed, some would say. Or a breed."

"The way they say it makes me want to punch them," Zach commented.

"It's not something a true friend would call you," Nate confirmed.

"Then I *will* punch them."

"Who has been calling you this?"

"Runs Fast, mostly, and a few that hang around with him."

"Runs Fast? Jumping Bull's boy?"

"Yep."

"How long has this been going on?"

"Oh, about ten sleeps, I reckon. Runs Fast has been picking on me every chance he gets lately. I don't know why. I've never done nothing to him."

"Why didn't you tell me sooner?"

There was a pause. "A man should always take care of his own problems. Isn't that what I heard you tell Uncle Shakespeare?"

Nate probed his memory for over half a minute before he recalled making such a statement, and he marveled that his son remembered the incident. It had been almost a year ago, during one of Shakespeare McNair's periodic visits to their cabin. McNair, his best friend and mentor, had been talking about a mutual acquaintance, a free trapper embroiled in a dispute with another man. Instead of confronting the offending party directly, the trapper had been trying to enlist the help of everyone he knew to side with him against his enemy. During the course of that conversation Nate had casually mentioned that any man worth his salt handled his own squabbles and didn't go around imposing on his friends.

"Isn't it?" Zach prompted.

"Yes, I do recollect saying something along those lines," Nate admitted. "But I was talking about grown men. It's perfectly all right for a boy your age to come to his folks when something like this happens."

"I'm not no whiner. I want to do what a man would do."

Nate looked over his shoulder and bestowed a kindly, knowing smile on his pride and joy. "You have a heap of growing to do, son, before you'll wear a man's britches. Don't rush things. These years are some of the best years of your life and you should enjoy them while they last."

"Why are these the best years?" the boy inquired.

"Because you don't have any responsibilities yet."

"I have my chores, don't I?" Zach said, sounding slightly offended. "I take care of the horses and chop wood and such."

"I'm not saying you don't do your fair share of the work," Nate assured him. "But it's a far cry from doing daily chores to having a wife and kids to keep fed and clothed and having a homestead to look after. Some responsibilities are bigger than others, and a wife and children are the biggest a man can have. He has to work real hard to give them the things he thinks they should have, and sometimes it can be almighty trying."

"Don't you like looking after Ma and me?"

Nate stopped until Zach came alongside him, and tenderly placed his hand on the boy's shoulder. "What a silly notion. Nothing in this whole wide world gives me greater pleasure than having to do for your ma and you. I never knew what genuine happiness was until I met Winona, and when you came along we were as happy as could be."

Zach pondered a bit. "If you like young'uns so much, how come I don't have any brothers or sisters?"

"The Lord knows we've tried, son," Nate said, inwardly amazed at the convoluted twists the boy's reasoning sometimes took. Nate was also a little bothered by the question. Had he somehow given Zach cause to doubt his love, or was the query merely prompted by idle curiosity?

"Running Wolf has three brothers and two sisters. He says that's too many, that they pick on each other all the time." Zach's brow creased. "If Ma does have babies, I hope she doesn't have five at once."

"I doubt she will," Nate said with a straight face.

"You never know, Pa. Beaver Tail's dog had a litter of six pups, and Tall Horse's dog had eight."

Nate made a mental note to have a long talk with his son about affairs between the sexes at the first opportunity. They'd already had a few discussions, but clearly he hadn't covered all he should.

The aspens were much nearer. Nate rested his Hawken across his thighs and scoured the wall of vegetation for sign of the elk. He saw nothing, and his mind began to drift. Instead of concentrating exclusively on the matter at hand, he found himself wondering why Jumping Bull's son had taken to giving Zach a hard time. He knew Jumping Bull, but not well. They were on speaking terms and would greet one another if they passed in the village, but Jumping Bull had never been overly friendly toward him. In fact, now that he thought about it, Jumping Bull had always been strangely aloof, even cold. Why?

Suddenly Nate spied a moving patch of brown among the slender trunks of the aspens. A moment later he made out the outline of a bull elk walking slowly westward. Quickly he snapped the rifle to his shoulder and touched his thumb to the hammer. He had to elevate the barrel to compensate for the slope. Fixing a bead on a spot behind the elk's powerful front shoulders, he began to cock the Hawken.

"Pa! Look!"

At the strident shout the elk whirled and vanished in the undergrowth so swiftly there was no chance for Nate to fire. One instant it was there, the next it was gone. Exasperated at his son's mistake, he swung around. "Zach, haven't I taught you better than to yell when you're closing in on game?"

The boy was pointing at the valley below.

Immediately Nate spotted them, three mounted Indians traversing the valley floor from east to west. They had just crossed the stream and were in plain sight in the tall grass. Sunlight glittered off a long lance one held. From so high up he couldn't tell to which tribe they belonged.

"Are they Shoshones, you think?" Zach asked.

"There are no hunting parties in the area I know of," Nate said.

"Maybe they're hostiles, Pa. Maybe they're Blackfeet."

"They only travel this far south to raid, and when they raid they like to go on foot," Nate pointed out. "I doubt they're Blackfeet." But they could, he thought to himself, be from one of a half-dozen tribes who were bitter enemies of the Shoshones. Warriors who would try to kill Zach and him on sight.

Zach was excited. "Should we hide and wait to see if they're after us?"

"No," Nate said calmly, hiding his blossoming worry. Where there were three, there might be more, *many* more, and here he was alone with his young son.

"They're awful close to the elk trail. Maybe they're just hunting elk like we are."

"They could be," Nate allowed, although he didn't believe that was the case. He scanned the expanse of craggy mountain beyond the fluttering tops of the trees while gnawing on his lower lip, his every instinct telling him to get the hell out of there, to get his son to safety. "Stick close," he cautioned, and angled higher.

Constantly winding right and left to avoid thickly clustered trunks, Nate slowly made his way through the aspen belt and into sparse pines above. The ground became rockier. Every now and then a stone would be dislodged by one of their horses and clatter downward. The air felt cooler, growing even more so as they approached a blanket of snow crowning the ragged summit.

A solitary hawk soared over the crest and swooped down above them, then banked and glided to a lower elevation.

"Was that a red hawk?" Zach asked.

"I didn't pay attention," Nate said, his eyes on a promising notch several hundred yards to their right toward which he was gingerly picking his way. He had to skirt several talus slopes where their horses might slip and fall. Always he tried to stay in cover in case the Indians below were scouring the mountain for them.

The notch was above the snow line, situated at the apex of a steep slope. Nate thought it prudent to climb down, and had Zach do likewise. The gelding and Zach's mare were as surefooted as mountain goats, but he dared not risk an accident. If one of their animals went lame they would be hard pressed to elude pursuers. Taking the reins in his left hand, he worked his way upward, his knee-high moccasins finding scant purchase on the packed, slippery snow.

"This is the first time I've ever been up this high," Zach remarked breathlessly. "Everything looks so small down below. That stream looks like a string. And those Indians look like ants."

Indians? Nate twisted and held a palm over his eyes to shield them from the glare. Crossing an open tract between the valley floor and the trees on the lower slope were five warriors riding in single file, most with upturned faces. He could guess what they were doing: searching the mountain for Zach and him. "We'd better hurry," he suggested, increasing his pace.

Soon they were at the notch, which proved to be, as Nate has hoped, a narrow pass to the opposite side of the mountain. There were plenty of elk, deer, and big-horn sheep tracks, none made recently.

Nate passed through the gap quickly, anxious to learn if there would be a way down the far slope. He feared the pass would open out on a towering cliff or an impassable gorge, which would force them to either retrace their steps down to the valley or to try and swing in a wide loop around the climbing Indians and pray they weren't discovered.

The first sight Nate beheld when he emerged from the shadowy pass was a cliff, thankfully off to the left and not barring their way. To his right grew dense forest. Directly below, the alpine fastness inclined gradually for hundreds of feet into more aspens. Nate and Zach mounted, and made their way toward them.

Zach seemed to have sensed Nate's urgency. The boy made no further comments until they were near the bottom. Then, craning his neck to see the pass, he said, "There's no sign of them yet, Pa."

"They'll show. Count on it," Nate said. From the heights he had sought, in vain, for a stream they could ride in for a few miles to throw the Indians off. Now he cut to the right into evergreens that would shield them from scrutiny from on high. He rode faster, heedless of the occasional branch that snatched at his clothing. Zach stayed right behind him, guiding the mare as adeptly as a seasoned mountain man.

Nate lost track of the many minutes spent in flight. Never once did he leave the sanctuary of the forest. Always he shunned clearings or breaks in the trees where they might be visible from the heights.

At length, as they negotiated the base of a curving hill, Nate changed direction and galloped to the top where massive, jumbled boulders afforded concealment for their tired mounts. It was the work of a moment to clamber onto a flat boulder and to go prone with the Hawken in both hands.

"Did we lose them?" Zach asked, lying down at his elbow.

"We'll soon know."

From their vantage point they could see for miles along their back trail. In the distance, silhouetted against the azure sky, was the pass, now no more than a dark slit at the crest of the mountain. The lower portions were blocked from view by intervening peaks and hills.

More minutes dragged by. Zach fidgeted and kept glancing apprehensively at Nate. Presently he made bold to state, "Maybe they weren't after us, Pa. Maybe we went to all this trouble for nothing."

Nate lifted his right arm, his forefinger extended, and heard Zach's intake of breath when his son saw the five stick figures that had appeared out of the notch. "Whoever they are, they're persistent," he said.

"They sure are taking their sweet time. I bet if we try, we can shake them," Zach said.

"You up to a little hard riding?"

"Try me."

"Then let's show them what the King men are made of," Nate proposed, giving his son a reassuring grin. "By the time we're through they'll wish they'd never laid eyes on our tracks."

Zachary laughed, delighted at the challenge confronting them. "Lead the way. And don't fret none about Mary. She can keep up with Pegasus easy except on the flats."

Mary was the mare. Pegasus was the pied gelding given to Nate by the grateful Nez Percé after he helped them rout a raiding party of Blackfeet. Neither horse balked when they were goaded into a gallop, and they swept down the hill with their manes and tails flying.

In all Nate's wide flung travels he had never visited this particular region before, but he had heard enough about it from Shoshones who had to readily recognize prominent landmarks and to keep his bearings as he made to the east with the intent of locating a fork of the Stinking River that must, by his estimation, lie eight to ten miles off.

Since speed was crucial, Nate didn't bother sticking to the shelter of the restricting trees any more. He favored the open stretches where their animals fairly flew. In their wake were tracks a greenhorn could follow, which would enable their pursuers to gain ground but not enough ground, Nate prayed, to overtake the two of them before they came to the river.

Trying not to be too obvious, Nate checked on Zach time and again. His pride swelled as he saw how splendidly the boy rode. He'd given his son numerous riding lessons and frequently watched Zach riding with other Shoshone boys, but not until now had he realized how expertly the boy could handle a horse. Begrudgingly, he admitted to himself that Zach was a much better rider than he had been at the same age—indeed, a better rider than he had been until his fateful trip west from New York City to the untamed frontier during his 19th year.

Part of the explanation for his son's ability had to be the one month out of every twelve spent with the Shoshones. Zach had learned skills he never would have mastered back in the States, where boys his age were subjected to dull days filled with the drudgery of schoolwork, or else were forced by economic necessity to work from dawn to dusk in order to contribute to the family welfare.

Sometimes Nate envied Zach. He wished his own childhood had been similarly spent amidst the primeval glory of the Rocky Mountains among a forthright people who lived simply by design rather than circumstance. People who took each day as it came, without fear of what tomorrow might bring. People who had few needs and fewer wants and who would gladly give the last piece of pemmican they had to a hungry stranger. Such were the Shoshones.

Mile after mile fell behind them as Nate reflected on his active years in the mountains and on the various hardships he had endured, hardships made bearable by the love of the woman who had claimed his heart. He shuddered to think how his life might have turned out had he never met Winona. Perhaps he would have gone back to New York and settled down to the accounting career his father had planned for him, to a boring existence of muddling over thick books crammed with meaningless figures under the critical eye of a penny-pinching employer. He would rather have died.

It was strange, Nate mused, the unforeseen turns a person's life could take. The whims of Fate were as unpredictable as mountain weather, changing with fickle abandon. One day a man might be on top of the world, the next living in the gutter. Of course, that was back in the States. In the wilderness the extremes were more basic. One day a man might be alive, the next dead.

And Nate would not have it any other way. Living from hand to mouth, never knowing one day what the next would bring, had caused him to appreciate the pleasures life had to offer that much more. Oddly enough, the never-ending dangers he daily faced from savage enemies and brutal beasts alike only added to his lust for life. It was as if he was a knife blade and the wilderness the whetstone on which he was being slowly but inexorably honed.

A sheer gully suddenly loomed in Nate's path, shattering his reverie. The gelding cleared the gulf in a single leap. Shifting, he saw the mare do the same and his son's beaming smile of triumph. "Well done," Nate cried.

The land had become more and more level, which was a good sign. Nate reckoned they were close to the Stinking River, so named by a wandering frontiersman who had taken part in the famed Lewis and Clark expedition to the Pacific Ocean, a man by the name of John Colter, undoubtedly the first white man to ever set foot in that part of the country.

The name, though, didn't do the river justice. From all Nate had heard it was one of the finest in the mountains. Colter, it so happened, had come on the river at the one spot where a large tar spring fouled the water and the air alike. Consequently, the unflattering designation.

Shortly Nate spied a winding strip of deciduous trees a mile further on. They turned out to be cottonwoods, willows, and others, types requiring much more water than evergreens and which normally grew along the banks of waterways. He was certain they bordered the river he sought, and within five minutes his conclusion was borne out when he drew rein beside the sluggish waters of the Stinking River.

"We'll rest here for a spell," he announced.

"Is it safe to do that, Pa?" Zach inquired.

Nate nodded as he swung to the ground. "We have quite a lead on those Indians. They might not even know that we know they're after us, in which case they'll take their sweet time trailing us so as not to give themselves away. We can afford a short rest." He indicated Pegasus and Mary. "We have to stop for their sakes, anyway. If our horses give out, those Indians will catch us for sure. Never forget, son, that a man must always think of his horse first and himself second."

"Always?"

Again Nate nodded. "Think of how hard it would be for us to make it back to the village without our horses. It would take forever, and we'd be tempting prey for every grizzly we met. Even a panther might see fit to attack us. A man left stranded afoot in this country is like a fish out of water. He has to be on his toes every second if he wants to stay alive."

While the stallion and the mare drank greedily under Zach's watchful care, Nate walked a short distance downriver, then retraced his steps and went an equal distance upriver. He checked the depth, the speed of the current, and the general lay of the land in both directions.

By the time Nate hurried back, the horses were done drinking and Zach was giving them a rubdown using handfuls of grass. "Those Indians are in for a surprise when they get here," he mentioned.

"Are you fixing to ambush them?"

"No. The odds are too great. I can't risk something happening to me." Climbing on Pegasus, Nate entered the water and turned upriver, staying close to the bank where the water only came up to his ankles.

Zach imitated Nate's example and declared, "I get it, Pa. They won't be able to track us from here on out."

The river was flowing just fast enough to swirl away any mud raised by the hoofs of their animals. Although

23

cold, the water wasn't frigid enough to be uncomfortable. Nate hugged the side for over two hours, at last riding out onto a wide bench covered with gently waving grass.

"What now, Pa?"

"We let the horses graze, then go pick a spot to camp and turn in early so we get a good night's sleep. Tomorrow we're going after elk again."

"But what if those Indians are still after us?"

"I doubt they'll come this far, son. But even if they do, it won't be until sometime tomorrow. There's not enough daylight left for them to reach this spot before dark. If and when they do, we'll be long gone."

Zachary giggled. "I have to hand it to you, Pa. You sure outfoxed them. They'll never catch us now."

"That's the idea, son," Nate said, matching his son's grin, extremely pleased with himself and delighted at the impression he had made on Zach. Thanks to his cleverness, they were safe. Or were they? whispered a tiny voice at the back of his mind, a voice he ignored with a shake of his head. There was such a thing as being too cautious, and he wasn't about to become that. Tomorrow they would down an elk, and in a few days they would head home. It would be as simple as that.

Or would it? asked the tiny voice.

Chapter Two

"There is something strange about these tracks."

Rolling Thunder glanced up from the leg of succulent roast venison on which he had been chewing and stared at Bobcat, who was kneeling on the soft ground close to the river. The flickering light from their crackling fire revealed Bobcat's puzzled expression. "What is strange?" Rolling Thunder asked.

"See for yourself."

Standing, Rolling Thunder wiped his greasy left hand on his leggings and walked over. The footprints here were much clearer than those he had seen by the stream that morning, so clear he had been able to tell the style of stitching used in the construction of the moccasins. Since no two tribes in the entire Rockies made their moccasins exactly alike, from the stitching and the shapes of the soles he had confirmed that the pair they pursued were indeed Shoshones. "Now what bothers you about them?" he inquired.

"Take a look," Bobcat said, touching a finger to the toes of several tracks left by the man.

At first Rolling Thunder noticed nothing unusual. Then, abruptly, he realized what he had missed detecting before and his blood raced through his veins. "One of them is a white man!" he exclaimed.

The shout brought Little Dog, Loud Talker, and Walking Bear from the fire on the run.

"What is this about a white man?" Little Dog wanted to know.

It was Bobcat who answered, accenting his words by tapping one of the footprints. "The man's toes point outward. We all know what that means."

Little Dog crouched to study the tracks, thinking quickly. Yes, he did know that only white men walked thus; Indians always walked with their toes pointing inward. It was yet another example of the truth that whites always did everything backwards. But if Bobcat was right it did not bode well for their hunting trip. One look at the sparkling gleam in Rolling Thunder's dark eyes justified his concern, so he spoke before anyone else. "The toes do not point outward all the time."

"Then it is a white man who has lived among Indians and has practiced walking correctly but doesn't always do so," Bobcat said.

"Or it could be a Shoshone with a limp," Little Dog suggested. If he could convince the others, they might refuse to go along with the idea Rolling Thunder was bound to soon propose.

"There is no evidence of a limp," Bobcat stated. "I tell you it is a white man and a Shoshone boy."

"Or," Rolling Thunder said, "a white man and his half-breed son. I seem to remember hearing about a white dog who is living with the northern Shoshones."

"All of us heard the story," Walking Bear interjected. "Don't you remember? It was four winters ago when we camped for a time with some Blackfeet. They told us about a white with powerful medicine who escaped from their clutches and in doing so killed one of their greatest warriors, White Bear." He paused. "They told us this white's name but it eludes me."

"Grizzly Killer," Loud Talker practically shouted. "They claim he has killed more of the giant bears than any man, Indian or white. They say he kills grizzlies as easily as other men kill flies."

Rolling Thunder smiled and gestured at the tracks with the leg bone. "Yes! I remember now! This must be him. The fierce Grizzly Killer." He said the last with marked contempt.

"We do not know that for certain," Little Dog said. "The Shoshones have other white friends. It could be any one of them."

"What does it really matter if it is Grizzly Killer or not? He is *white*," Rolling Thunder said.

"And that is all that is important," Little Dog said sarcastically.

Pivoting, Rolling Thunder swept them with his gaze. "Friends, what do we care about a few paltry elk when we have the chance to kill a hated white? Our wives can wait a while longer for the meat. Just think of the praise they will heap on us if one of us takes this man's scalp back."

Bobcat stood. "It would be quite an honor, especially if this is Grizzly Killer. We would have done what the Blackfeet could not do."

"We can prove we are the better warriors," Loud Talker said, and vented a bloodthirsty war whoop. "I say we go after these two. If the boy is worthy, I will take him into my lodge and raise him as my own."

"If he is the son of Grizzly Killer I would like to take him into my own lodge," Walking Bear objected. "He should grow up to be a strong warrior with potent medicine, a credit to the man who rears him."

"I say we kill them both," Bobcat said. "That way two of us can count coup."

Little Dog listened to the ensuing heated discussion in disgusted silence. His friends were letting their yearning for glory sweep aside their common sense. None of them, apparently, had noticed that this Grizzly Killer, or whoever the man might be, was leading them back toward the heart of Shoshone country. Their quarry was no fool. If they continued on, the danger of running into a large Shoshone war party grew with each hour. Little Dog feared they might even be tricked into riding straight into a trap.

Rolling Thunder had heard enough about what to do with the boy. Clearing his throat to get their attention, he adopted a solemn air and said, "We can decide the boy's fate when we have caught him. As for the man, it is only a question of which one of us gets to him first. But we must be very careful. We must be on our guard for the Shoshones at all times. I, for one, do not plan to have my hair adorn a Shoshone's lance."

"Why worry?" Bobcat said. "We will be in and out of their country before they know it."

"So you hope," Little Dog told him. Perturbed, he walked to their fire and cut off a large chunk of meat to eat. Squatting with his back to the river, he nibbled and considered whether to waste his breath objecting to their new quest. The others weren't about to change their minds just because he had an uneasy feeling about proceeding. They would say his nerves were on edge, or joke he was losing his courage as they had done previously.

"Why are you not being very sociable this evening?"

Little Dog involuntarily stiffened. He hadn't heard Rolling Thunder approach. For so big a man, Rolling Thunder could move like a ghost when he wanted to. "I was hungry," Little Dog responded.

"What is troubling you, old friend?"

"Not a thing."

"Do you have so little respect for me now that you lie to me? What have I done to deserve such treatment?"

Annoyed, Little Dog spat softly. "You know very well what you have done. Your heart's desire has come true and you are going to risk all our lives hunting this white eyes."

"If you knew what was in my heart, why did you come along?"

"Need you ask?" Little Dog said, and crammed a large bite of juicy meat into his mouth. He nearly started when Rolling Thunder's hand fell on his shoulder.

"I have always valued your friendship most of all, Little Dog, because you see me as I am and still you count me as your friend. I knew you would guess the truth, but I also knew I could count on you to go along with what I wanted to do."

Little Dog had to tuck the meat against a cheek to talk. He intentionally held his voice to just above a whisper. "The others are fools, but I am a bigger fool than all of them put together because I know what could happen and I am too timid to protest."

"You can go back if you want. No one would hold it against you."

"Perhaps not. But none of them would understand." Little Dog turned on his heels and regarded Rolling Thunder critically. "They are my friends too. What manner of friend would I be if I deserted them when they need me the most? No, I will stay. I will go along with your scheme, and I hope for your sake that everything works out and White Buffalo is put in his place."

"He will be. I am risking my life to make it so."

"You are placing all of our lives in peril," Little Dog corrected him. "I only pray it is worth it."

David Thompson

* * *

Not quite 12 miles distant, nestled in a hollow where the whipping wind couldn't extinguish their tiny fire, Nate and Zach hunched over the last of the fish they had caught at dusk. Except for a few essentials such as ammunition and black powder, they had not brought any supplies along with them, not even jerky to munch on along the way. They had been living off the land ever since leaving the village, all part of Nate's plan to give his son a true taste of life in the wild reaches of the uncompromising mountains. If they wanted full bellies they had to snare game, and so far they had not gone hungry a single day.

"What do you reckon Ma is doing right about now?" the boy wondered.

"Probably visiting her cousin, Willow Woman. I swear those two are like two peas in a pod. You can hardly pry them apart once they take to jawing."

Zach chuckled and tried to sound mature as he said, "You sure have them pegged, Pa. I reckon you know more about women than Uncle Shakespeare said you do."

"Oh? And what did dear Uncle Shakespeare have to say?"

"Do you remember that big fight Ma and you had once over me going along on a raid into Ute country?"

"Your mother didn't want you to go, and I thought it might be good for you since all you were going to do was tend the horses and lay low if we ran into Utes," Nate recalled. "So?"

"So I asked Uncle Shakespeare why Ma and you argue like that sometimes even though you love each other. He said it's only natural. He said men and women can't help rubbing each other the wrong way now and then 'cause they're so different. Then he used a lot of those funny words from that big book he carries around all the time."

30

"He quoted from the works of Shakespeare."

"Yep."

"When did he mention me?"

"When I asked what all those funny words had to do with Ma and you. He said you're still young so you don't rightly know much about women and it's not your fault if you get Ma riled now and then. He said your life is"— Zach thought for a few seconds—"a comedy of errors, whatever that is, and then he laughed so hard his face turned beet red."

"Remind me to pay your uncle a visit when we get back."

"Can we? I'd like that, Pa. He's a lot of fun to be around."

Nate spread out their blankets side by side, then strolled over to where their horses were tethered. Pegasus was grazing. The mare stood with her head bowed and her eyes closed. He patted the gelding, and scanned the adjacent forest while listening intently to the various night sounds around them. An owl posed its eternal question. A wolf wailed a lonesome lament far to the west. To the south, faint but unmistakable, arose the throaty snarl of a prowling panther, and Nate waited to see if it would be repeated so he might get some idea of which direction the panther was moving. But the big cat didn't cooperate.

After a while Nate walked toward the fire. He wasn't particularly worried about the panther since the solitary cats rarely attacked humans or went after livestock in the close proximity of humans. The horses should be safe. Even if the panther did venture near, he was confident the keen ears and nose of the gelding would detect its presence and that Pegasus would act up something awful, thereby awakening him.

The fire had burned low. Reddish-orange tongues of flame licked at the few pieces of wood not yet charred. Zach, exhausted from the many hours spent in the saddle, had already curled up and appeared to be sound asleep.

Nate gazed fondly at his son, feeling all warm inside. The boy tried so hard and did so well. Suddenly he saw a vague shape gliding out of the inky shadows toward Zach and he froze. The dancing firelight illuminated a low-slung creature on all fours. He glimpsed a hairy, triangular face framed by high, pointed ears and a long nose held close to the ground. For a second Nate thought it must be a wolf, and his right hand streaked to one of the two flintlocks wedged under his wide leather belt on either side of his metal buckle. As he took hasty aim the animal took another stride closer and was bathed in more firelight, allowing Nate to see that it wasn't a wolf after all.

Their visitor was a coyote.

Mystified, Nate held his fire. Coyotes were not noted for their ferocity, and this one gave no sign of being about to pounce. Rather, it seemed more curious than anything else as it slunk steadily closer to Zach. Nate could see its nose twitching as it tested the air, getting the boy's scent.

Abruptly, Zach shifted, rolling onto his back and uttering a low moan as he did. The coyote reacted as if shot, recoiling and wheeling to vanish in the brush with nary a sound.

Nate stuck the flintlock back under his belt, and returned to the blankets to take a seat next to his son. He scoured the shroud of darkness, but the coyote was long gone. Reflecting on its odd behavior, he thought of his wife and how, if she had been there, she would say the incident had been an omen. Like all Shoshones she was quite superstitious, reading meanings into everyday events that Nate tended to shrug off as simple happenstance. But it *was* strange, he conceded, that Zach, whose given Shoshone name was Stalking Coyote, should be visited by a wild coyote in the dead of night.

Shrugging, Nate positioned his Hawken next to his right side, and lay down on his back so he could gaze at the myriad of brilliant stars on high. Few spectacles inspired his soul like the celestial tapestry that nightly adorned the heavens. It was a time to lie quietly and think, to ponder what had happened during the day and plan for tomorrow.

He thought about the five Indians and hoped they had given up the chase. Many times in the past he had lost pursuers by taking to water as he had done today, so he was optimistic the five wouldn't pick up the trail again. Still, he would have to be vigilant for a while.

A twig snapped in the brush.

Nate smiled and held himself still. The coyote had come back, and he didn't want to do anything that would scare it off. He was interested to learn how close it would venture if he pretended to be asleep.

A second twig cracked.

Ever so slowly, Nate twisted his head, his eyes nearly shut, and waited for the animal to appear. An indistinct shape moved at the limits of his vision and he heard a loud crunch. For a coyote, the critter was uncommonly noisy. He had to suppress a laugh when it made yet another sound.

Gradually the indistinct shape solidified into a black mass, a huge black mass, an enormous lumbering bulk that strode fearlessly forward into the last of the light from the fire and grunted as if in surprise on finding two humans in its domain.

Nate's breath caught in his throat and his blood changed to ice. A shiver rippled down his spine. His right hand rested on the barrel of the Hawken, but he dared not try to use the rifle since he couldn't hope to put a ball into the monster standing in front of him before it ripped him apart with its giant claws. Even if, by some miracle, he did, it

33

was rare that a single shot dispatched a full-grown grizzly.

The bear swung its ponderous head from side to side while sniffing loudly. Perhaps it smelled the lingering odor of the cooked fish, or perhaps another scent attracted it. Whatever, the grizzly stepped forward until its great head hung directly above the two figures on the ground.

Nate could feel its warm, fetid breath on his face and see the underside of its chin. From where he lay the bear resembled a living mountain of solid muscle. Within a foot of his face was a gigantic paw, the claws glistening dully. A drop of drool splattered on Nate's cheek but he ignored it.

Grunting, the bear nosed the man and the boy. The latter mumbled and fidgeted and the bear cocked its head, its cavernous mouth opening and closing. The scent of the morsel was tantalizing, but the grizzly had eaten half an hour ago and its stomach was full. Too, the bear had never seen anything like these two creatures, and it still remembered the bitter lesson it had learned at an early age when it tried to eat another creature it had never encountered before, a creature covered with long, sharp quills that had cut into its nose and mouth and had taken weeks to tear loose, causing no end of pain.

Nate saw the grizzly staring at Zach, and braced for the worst. His left hand inched to the tomahawk on his hip, and he started to ease the weapon free. He would undoubtedly be crushed to a pulp, but he was not about to lie there and let the monster devour his son. The wooden handle felt small against his palm, the weapon itself puny. Girding his courage, he tensed to leap erect and swing.

All of a sudden the bear backed up, spun, and shuffled off, plowing through the brush with all the finesse of a steam engine. The crashing and crackling grew progressively fainter until they were smothered by distance.

Nate sat bolt upright, his heart thumping in his chest. That, he told himself, had been too damn close for comfort! He looked at his peacefully slumbering son, and was so relieved that tears formed at the corners of his eyes. Then he quickly rose and gathered more fuel for the fire, bringing back a half-dozen loads of broken branches, enough to make a waist-high pile.

Not in the least sleepy, Nate fed wood to the few remaining flames until he had a roaring blaze going. From where he squatted he could see the horses, and he marveled that the grizzly had not caught their scent and that neither horse had whinnied in fright during its brief stay. Shaking his head in amazement, he verified that his two pistols, the tomahawk, and his butcher knife were all in place about his waist. The Hawken went across his lap. He sat up until near midnight, dreading that the grizzly might see fit to wander back, but the forest lay tranquil under a moonless sky.

Despite his best efforts, Nate's weary body succumbed to the inevitable. His eyes closed. He reclined on his side, the rifle in his hands, and decided to sleep a little while, just enough to refresh him. Then he'd build the fire up once more and keep watch over his son until daylight. That was all he needed. A few hours' rest.

The sharp neigh of a terrified horse slashed into Nate's consciousness like a hot knife through butter and he came instantly awake. He was upright and glancing every which way before he quite realized what had awakened him. The mare whinnied, providing an answer, and he heard both horses restlessly moving back and forth.

From the deep woods came a guttural growl.

For a second Nate believed the grizzly had returned and was about to attack their mounts; then the growl lengthened and grew louder, becoming a drawn-out, savage snarl such as only the largest of cats could utter. It was a panther, perhaps the same panther he had heard previously!

"Zach!" Nate said as he scooped up the Hawken. "Wake up, son. We have trouble on our hands."

The boy tossed and his eyelids fluttered.

"Wake up!" Nate urged, fearful the beast would spring before they reached their mounts. He prodded his son with his toe. "Come on!"

"Pa?" Zach said uncertainly, sitting up. He looked around in confusion. "What is it? What's the matter?"

"Panther," Nate explained. "Grab your gun and follow me."

Young Zach came to full alertness as the tension in his father's tone conveyed the danger confronting them. He grabbed the long rifle lying beside him, the first and only rifle he had ever owned, given to him by his parents just a few short weeks before the elk hunt began, and jumped to his feet.

"Stay close," Nate cautioned, treading warily toward Pegasus and Mary. Both animals stood stock-still, staring intently into the darkened woods to the north of where they were tied. He wondered why the cat had snarled the way it had since usually panthers were quiet when stalking prey, and he gave silent thanks that this cat was the exception rather than the rule. Had it approached noiselessly, by now one of their horses would be dead.

"Where is it, Pa?" Zach whispered, his small thumb on the cool metal hammer. He tried to keep his voice steady so his father wouldn't suspect how scared he felt. His mouth was dry, his palms damp.

"It could be anywhere," Nate responded. "Keep your eyes peeled."

Zach absently nodded, his mind whirling so that he couldn't think straight and didn't realize his father, being in front of him, couldn't see his head move. He scanned the line of trees on both sides, the dark, ominous trunks not more than ten feet off on either side, and remembered the many tales he had heard about how far panthers could leap. What if the cat charged his pa or him instead of the horses? It would be on them before they could get off a shot. The thought spawned terror that spread like wildfire throughout his body, causing an odd burning sensation on his skin and making his limbs tingle as if they were asleep.

Pegasus had raised his head to sniff the breeze. His front hoof stamped the ground hard twice and then he moved a yard to the left, his big eyes locked on the bole of a large tree in the forest directly across from him.

Nate could guess why. The Hawken cocked, he moved around the horses until he was between the gelding and the tree. "Get set, son," he said softly. "If it's going to attack, it won't wait long."

Zach, struck dumb by his terror, made no reply, and he saw his father glance at him. At the very same instant he saw something else: the panther, its claws extended, its razor teeth exposed, vaulting from concealment straight at them.

Chapter Three

To one who has never experienced raw, unbridled fear, the first time can be virtually paralyzing. There had been times in the past when young Zach had been afraid, but he had never, ever known such stark fright as that which seized him at the moment the panther sprang. He wanted to cry out, to warn his father, but his vocal chords had changed to stone. He wanted to raise the Kentucky rifle and fire, but his arms were frozen in place. All he could do was watch helplessly as the huge cat sailed gracefully through the air.

Nate was not taken completely unawares, however. He'd seen his son's eyes widen, and he pivoted toward the forest just as the panther slammed into him. By sheer chance he had the Hawken at chest height, so it was the rifle the cat's slashing forepaws struck instead of his body. Nate was spared from being ripped wide open. The impact, though, sent him stumbling backwards into Pegasus.

Hissing like a venomous serpent, the panther crouched and gathered its leg muscles to jump again.

At last Zach found his voice. Horrified by the mental image of the panther sinking its teeth into his father, a heartfelt *"No!"* burst from his thin lips.

Distracted, the big cat looked at him.

And it was then that Nate, having recovered his balance, hastily pointed the Hawken at the panther's head. His finger was tightening on the trigger when the courageous gelding, which was eager to close with the intruder, tried to get past him, jostling him roughly as it did and inadvertently jarring the barrel to one side. The Hawken thundered, but the ball missed by inches.

Swiftly Nate clawed at a flintlock, hoping against hope he would be able to fire before the cat pounced. The blast and the cloud of smoke had momentarily startled the panther into immobility, and he knew the spell wouldn't last long. It didn't. Just as the flintlock was clearing his belt, the cat snarled, whirled, and flashed into the undergrowth.

Nate extended his arm, but there was no target to hit. He listened, yet heard only the wind. Slowly he lowered the pistol as it dawned on him that the crisis was past. The panther had been scared off and wasn't about to bother them again.

"Is it gone, Pa?" Zach asked timidly.

"Yep." Nate studied the boy's ashen features and mustered a lopsided grin. "Gave you a bit of a fright, did it?"

Zach gulped and nodded.

"Happens to all of us at one time or another. It's nothing to be ashamed of."

"I'll bet you weren't afraid."

"There wasn't time for me to be scared. It all happened so fast."

Nate took a minute to reload the Hawken, then stroked each of the horses in turn, speaking softly to them to calm them down. Presently he headed for the fire, his son, head bowed, at his side. "Are you all right, Zach?"

"I'm fine, Pa," Zach lied, because his emotions were in seething turmoil. He felt so bad he wanted to crawl into a hole and die. The way he saw it, he had behaved like a coward. And in his estimation there was no worse fate in all the word than being yellow.

To Shoshone men, courage was everything, the most essential of manly traits. Some of Zach's earliest memories were of Shoshone warriors recounting the brave deeds they had done to earn the coups they had counted. Countless times he had listened in rapt fascination as Touch the Clouds, Spotted Bull, Drags the Rope, and others told of their daring exploits, and always he longed for the day when he would perform deeds to match or exceed theirs.

As if that wasn't unsettling enough, for years Zach had heard stories about his father, about the many grizzlies his pa had slain and the many foes his pa had killed in defense of the tribe. At least a half-dozen times various warriors had said that Grizzly Killer was one of the bravest men alive. More than once Zach had been told that he was a lucky boy to have such a stalwart father, and that when he grew up he must do his father proud by being equally as courageous.

And look at what had happened! Zach reflected sourly. He'd had a chance to show just how brave he was, and instead he had discovered that at heart he was a coward. He'd let his pa down and himself down. How could he ever hope to make his pa proud when he had no courage at all? His lower lip trembled as he held back the tears dampening the corners of his eyes, and he was glad his father couldn't see his face as he lay down on his side with his arms wrapped around the Kentucky rifle.

"You get some more sleep, son," Nate remarked. "I'll keep watch a spell."

"I'll try."

"Are you sure you're not feeling poorly? You sound as if you're coming down with a cold."

"I never felt better, Pa," Zach said, and then, under his breath, he repeated bitterly, "Never felt better."

The barking of a dog brought Winona out of her peaceful sleep. Snug and warm under a thick, soft buffalo robe, she rolled onto her back and stretched languidly while gazing up through the open smoke flap at the top of the lodge. A pink hue tinged the sky, signifying dawn was not far off.

Winona's instinctive reaction was to start to rise so she could prepare breakfast for her husband and son. Then, grinning at her forgetfulness, she sank down and tucked the robe up under her chin. Her beloved Nate and dearest Zach would not return for six or seven sleeps yet. She could sleep as long as she wanted. Why, she might even scandalize herself in the eyes of the other women and not get up until after sunrise. They would think she was becoming lazy.

The notion made her giggle.

Winona thought of her husband and son and wished them well. By now, according to the plans Nate had laid out for her before their departure, they should be well up in the mountains in an area where elk were as plentiful as chipmunks, having the time of their lives. She was glad she had talked her husband into doing it. Zach, in her opinion, was long overdue to learn those skills that would serve him in excellent stead as he grew to full manhood. He was already eight; by the same age most Shoshone boys were competent hunters and knew how to butcher a variety of game without wasting a shred of meat.

Voices sounded outside, those of women going to the nearby river for water. Somewhere a child laughed.

Throwing back the buffalo robe, Winona stood. Old habits were hard to break, and since she had been rising before daylight every day of her life, she felt uncomfortable doing otherwise. Life was meant for living, not for wasting. She wanted to attend to certain chores so she could visit her cousin, Willow Woman.

Shortly Winona emerged from the lodge, her lithe figure adorned in a beaded buckskin dress and moccasins. A large tin pan, 18 inches in diameter, was clutched in her bronzed left hand. The wind whipped her long raven hair as she strolled across the open space to the river and knelt.

"How is the wife of Grizzly Killer this day?"

Winona looked up into the smiling face of Rabbit Woman, who was short and unusually plump for a Shoshone, and who seldom spoke to Winona unless she had a sarcastic comment to make. The two had known each other since childhood but had never gotten along. "I am well. How is the wife of Knife in Hand?"

"Very tired," Rabbit Woman answered, squatting so she could dip the water bucket she held into the river. Made from a buffalo paunch, it had a leather strap for a handle that she clasped tightly as the bucket slowly filled. "My brother showed up at our lodge well before the sun came up and wanted my help in cutting up a buck he had shot."

"He should have cut it up himself," Winona said politely in sympathy while lowering the pan into the river.

"You know how Jumping Bull is," Rabbit Woman said. "He was in a hurry."

Winona had to use both hands to steady the pan, which became heavier by the moment. She listened with half an ear as her companion went on.

"It is sad that Jumping Bull has not found a new wife to take the place of Eagle Shawl. A man should not live his life alone. And too, his son, Runs Fast, needs a mother."

"True," Winona said, being polite.

"Jumping Bull is a great warrior. He has twelve coup to his credit, and three of them were Blackfeet he killed with just his knife. Any woman would be proud to have him as her husband."

"I am sure he will find another wife," Winona said as she lifted the pan out.

"He has his eyes on someone who appeals to him, although what he sees in her I do not know. I have tried to talk him out of courting her, but he will not listen. Men can be so stubborn at times."

At this Winona grinned. "Men are stubborn *all* the time," she joked, and had started to leave when Rabbit Woman put a hand on her arm.

"I want you to know I argued against the idea until I was hoarse from talking, but he would not listen. When Jumping Bull sets his mind to something, nothing can change it. Many others will be angry at what he does, but that will not stop him. It would be better for all if the woman he wants moves into his lodge without causing trouble."

Mildly surprised that Rabbit Woman was confiding in her, Winona replied, "Jumping Bull is fortunate to have a sister who cares so much." She began to turn, but Rabbit Woman restrained her.

"I do care. I care with all my heart. He has always treated me kindly and helped me when I needed help. I can do no less for him, can I?"

"I suppose not," Winona said.

Opening her mouth as if to say more, Rabbit Woman evidently changed her mind, let go of Winona, and hurried off, walking so fast she spilled some of the water from her bucket. Soon she was lost among the lodges.

Winona ambled toward her own lodge. She was even more baffled, but she decided Rabbit Woman's problems were none of her affair. Behind her the golden crest of the sun peeked above the horizon. In the trees beyond the encampment birds were greeting the new day with their customary chorus. She passed several friends and exchanged pleasantries. To the south her uncle, Spotted Bull, stepped out into the sunlight and waved to her. All she could do, with her hands burdened by the pan, was smile back.

So preoccupied was Winona by the sights and sounds of the stirring village that she was only 15 feet from her lodge when she spotted something lying on the ground in front of the entrance. Eyes narrowing, she drew near enough to identify what it was and promptly halted, in shock, the full implication hitting her with the force of a physical blow. Now she understood why Rabbit Woman had sought her out. Now she knew why the woman had confided in her. A cold wind seemed to chill her to the marrow and she shuddered.

For there on a square piece of hide rested the haunch of a recently slain deer.

"We are wasting our time," Little Dog commented testily with a gesture at the river swirling past to his right. "There is no sign of where the two of them left the water. Why bother going on with this when our wives can use the elk meat we supposedly came after?"

Rolling Thunder, who rode a few yards ahead, snapped a look over his broad shoulder. "Are you saying I lied to you and the others?" he challenged.

Sighing, Little Dog gazed across the river at the opposite shore where Walking Bear, Bobcat, and Loud Talker were all scouring the ground for tracks their quarry might have left. They knew that the man and the child had gone up the river, but as yet they had been unable to find the spot where the pair took to the land again.

"I asked you a question," Rolling Thunder said, his voice low and hard.

Little Dog would rather have avoided the issue entirely, but since Rolling Thunder was so touchy about it, he reasoned that clearing the air would be best for all. "No," he said in resignation. "You did not deliberately lie to us. You truly intended to hunt elk." He paused. "Yet if that was all you planned to do, we would not have needed to travel so far from our own country. You insisted on traveling here to hunt. Why? Are the elk here fatter than they are in our own country? No. Are they easier to find? Perhaps. But in the back of your mind you have been hoping to find something else. You knew there are more white men in this region than elsewhere, and above all else you hope to count coup on one before we return to our people."

"And you hold this against me?"

"Not really, because I know why you do it. You want to be chief one day. The only other warrior who might dispute you is White Buffalo, who is just as brave as you are and has almost as many scalps hanging in his lodge as you do in yours." Little Dog spied a large trout out in the water and watched it swim lazily by. Oh, that he might be a fish and not have to contend with the ambitions of vain friends! "There is one big difference between the two of you, though. White Buffalo has the scalp of a white trapper; you do not. And so you want to add one to your collection so that he will not be able to stand up before our people and claim an honor that you do not have."

"*I* should be the next chief, not him," Rolling Thunder declared, striking his chest in his passion. "He sees himself as a mighty warrior, yet he is not half the man that I am."

"So you will do whatever is necessary to match his feats," Little Dog said rather sadly.

"Would you do otherwise if you' were me?"

"I am not you so I cannot say."

In silence they rode on as the sun climbed steadily, warming the crisp mountain air. Rolling Thunder made no more mention of his true motive for venturing into Shoshone territory, but secretly he vowed that he was going to track the man and the boy down if it took an entire moon to do. Counting coup on a white man would increase his standing in the tribe to where no one, not even the redoubtable White Buffalo, could prevent him from assuming the mantle of leadership.

A sudden shout from the opposite bank drew Rolling Thunder's attention to Walking Bear, who was grinning and jabbing a finger to the northeast. Rolling Thunder looked. Then his mouth curled in elation.

Several miles away, spiraling skyward, was the pale gray smoke from a camp fire.

"I could sure use another piece of jerky, Pa."

Nate rummaged in the parfleche at his feet and handed over a strip of the dried, salted meat to his Zach. "This makes the sixth one. Sometimes I swear that you have a bottomless pit for a stomach."

Zach's face lit up, the first time all day, and he replied, "I take after you. Ma said so herself. And Uncle Shakespeare told me that you're the only man he knows who can eat a whole bull buffalo at one sitting."

"He should talk. Remind me to tell you about the time he drank the Yellowstone River dry."

"He did not," Zach said, and laughed.

"Just ask the Shoshones," Nate said, overjoyed that the boy was finally showing his customary spark. All morning Zach had been inexplicably moody and had never spoken unless addressed, which was so unusual that Nate, remembering the nasal twang in his son's voice the previous night, had twice checked his son's forehead to see if Zach had a fever and might be coming down with something.

Well shy of noon Nate had been inspired to call a halt to their ride so they could eat and he could down a few cups of hot coffee. So little sleep had he gotten after the panther attack that he needed the coffee to stay awake. Three hot cups had invigorated him, and he was ready to resume their hunt.

The fire had about died down anyway. A tendril of smoke wafted upward as Nate poked the embers with a stick, extinguishing the last tiny flame. "Always remember to put out your camp fires," he remarked for the boy's benefit. "A careless spark can start a raging fire which could burn for days, maybe weeks. And always build your fires small, like the Indians do, so there's less chance of an enemy spotting it."

"Anything else?" Zach asked, enthused to learn more. As with most children, his irrepressible spirit could not stay smothered forever. For the time being he had shut last night's cowardice from his mind.

"Yes," Nate said. "Have you noticed how I always arrange the branches for our fires?"

Zach nodded. "You put them down like the spokes in a wagon wheel instead of piling them on top of each other."

"It's the Indian way of making fires. The woods burns slower so you don't have to gather as much to last you. It also burns steadier, which makes it easier to keep the flames under control."

"So that's why they do it that way," Zach said thoughtfully.

"You've got to keep in mind," Nate elaborated as he discarded the tiny bit of coffee left in the pot, "the Indians have been living in the wild for a long time.

47

They're masters at woodcraft. It's safe to say they've forgotten more over the years than our own people will ever learn. They treat Nature with respect instead of contempt. Pay attention and learn all you can because you never know when what you learn will come in handy."

Shortly they were on the go again, Zach on Nate's left. "Pa, you lived a long time back in the States. Which is better, the white way of life or the Indian way of life?"

The question caught Nate off guard. He pondered a minute, not caring to say anything that would embitter his son toward the society of white men. His own decision along those lines had been made the day he took Winona as his wife, but he wanted Zach to one day make up his own mind. So he said, "They both have their merits."

"But which is the best?" the boy asked with the single-minded persistence of the very young.

"I suppose the answer depends on what a person wants out of life," Nate said. "If safety and security is what you're after, then the white man's life is best. East of the Mississippi you hardly ever have to worry about being set on by hostiles, and since they've killed off all the grizzlies and most of the wolves and panthers, you'd never have to fret about those either. Stores nowadays carry ready-made clothes, so you'd never have to bother with sewing your own buckskins together. And with all the restaurants and saloons and taverns and such, you'd hardly ever have to cook your own food. There'd always be somewhere you could eat if you had the price."

"The white way of life sure sounds easy."

"That it does, but the easy way isn't always the best way."

"How so?"

"Life was never meant to be easy, Zach. Take a good look around you sometime. See how every creature in the mountains has to struggle to survive." Nate indicated a circling eagle to the south. "Wild animals have to work hard if they want to live. They spend their days hunting or foraging or seeking water, and the whole time they have to be on the lookout for their enemies because if they let down their guard for just a short while, they could wind up dead. But does all this hardship make them sickly? On the contrary. Most of them are as sleek and healthy as they could be."

Zach was listening attentively.

"The only animals that have it easy are those that have all their needs taken care of by man. Take cows and pigs, for instance. They have it about the easiest of any animals anywhere. All they do is stand around and eat all day, growing fatter and lazier as they get older and older. The same holds true for men and women. If we have it too easy, we grow fat and lazy just like cows and pigs."

"I see," Zach said. He regarded his father with frank admiration. "Tarnation, Pa. You sure know a lot. I bet you're the smartest man around."

"Not quite," Nate said, and chuckled.

Half a mile was covered before Zach broached another question that showed how deeply he had been thinking about his father's words. "I'd rather be a mountain lion than a cow any day. Why do folks wants things so easy?"

"Because they're afraid to take risks, I imagine. They don't want anything to do with something that might upset the orderly lives they like to live." Nate arched his spine to relieve a kink. "Most of them work at dull jobs where they do the same thing day after day, month after month, year after year, and earn just enough money to get by. But they put up with the drudgery because they can fill their bellies three times a day and wear new clothes now and then and have a roof over their heads."

"And they're happy living like that?"

"That's the strange part, son. Most of them say they're not all that happy, but they won't lift a finger to change things."

A few more yards fell behind them.

"If you don't mind, Pa, I figure I'd like to live in the mountains the rest of my life. City living doesn't sound like something I'd be interested in."

"It's your choice," Nate said, realizing he had done exactly what he hadn't wanted to do and inadvertently influenced his son's thinking. He shifted, and was about to point out some good aspects of white culture when to their rear there arose a succession of crackling and crunching sounds as something crashed through the brush directly toward them.

Chapter Four

Winona saw a shadow fall across the open flap of the lodge, and glanced down at the butcher knife lying partially concealed under a folded blanket at her side. The hilt was within easy reach. Girding herself, she looked at the entrance and the husky man squatting there, keeping her features composed. "This is an honor, Jumping Bull," she said pleasantly.

The warrior, attired in his finest buckskins, his hair braided and adorned with several feathers, scowled and rested a hand on the deer haunch. "You did not touch this."

"It is not mine," Winona said, devoting herself to the pair of Zach's leggings she was mending.

"I left it for you."

"I know."

"Then you should have claimed it."

Pausing in the act of using her buffalo-bone sewing

awl, Winona met his gaze. "My husband provides for me. There was no need for you to take it on yourself to share your kill with us."

Jumping Bull poked his head inside and started to ease his wide shoulders and chest through the opening. Almost as an afterthought, he asked, "May I enter?"

"No."

The man stopped, but made no move to back up. "I need to talk to you," he declared.

"You may talk to me from outside. My ears work quite well and I will hear everything you say."

"This is foolish," Jumping Bull said gruffly, lifting a foot inside and beginning to straighten.

"No!" Winona's voice rang out so loudly that she was heard 20 yards away.

Again Jumping Bull stopped, his expression becoming one of baffled annoyance. A look behind him showed a number of men, women, and children who were studying him curiously. Since to enter a lodge uninvited was a serious breach of tribal etiquette, he sank back on his heels just beyond the flap. "You are being most inconsiderate," he chided. "All I want is to tell you what is on my mind."

"Of what interest are your thoughts to me?" Winona countered disdainfully.

"They will be, once you know them," Jumping Bull predicted. "I have decided the time is ripe for me to take another wife, and I have chosen you."

A merry laugh tinkled from Winona's throat. "You are forgetting that I already have a husband."

"A white man is no fit husband for a beautiful woman like you. You are a full-blooded Shoshone. You should have a full-blooded Shoshone as a mate."

Bristling at the insult against Nate, Winona hid her feelings and commented, "I am quite content to be the woman of Grizzly Killer. He is a great warrior who cares for his family very much. No man could make me happier."

"I could," Jumping Bull asserted. "And I have decided you will come live with me this very day. So pack your things and we will go."

Winona set down the awl, her right hand drifting to the smooth hilt of the butcher knife. "It seems to me that you are making a lot of decisions concerning others without first consulting them. I have no desire to live with you, Jumping Bull. I love Grizzly Killer."

"You will forget him in time. Come." He beckoned her.

"No."

"I can easily drag you out if you continue to be so stubborn. Remember, you have no father or brothers to defend you. And the dog you call a husband is gone."

"I will be certain to tell him you said that," Winona said, maintaining her calm demeanor with difficulty. She refused to let him know how rattled she was by the dreadful conflict that was brewing. "And as for protectors, you should remember that my uncle, Spotted Bull, is close by, and that he has regarded me as he does his own daughter since the deaths of my parents."

"Spotted Bull will mind his own business," Jumping Bull said. "He will see that this is between the white dog and me."

"Can you be sure of that?" Winona asked. "And what about his son, Touch the Clouds, who is not only my cousin but one of the best friends my husband has? Will he stand by and do nothing while you mistreat me?" She detected a hint of indecision in the man's dark eyes, and knew that mentioning the name of the most renowned of all Shoshone warriors had had the desired effect.

Touch the Clouds was aptly named. He was a giant standing almost seven feet high and endowed with a massive physique to match his towering height, and his prowess in warfare was legendary among his people.

Winona went on. "And do not forget my husband's many other friends. Drags the Rope, Lone Wolf, He Who Rides Standing—none of them will like my being bothered while he is away."

"They have no right to interfere," Jumping Bull said petulantly. "This is my affair, not theirs." He shifted his weight from one heel to the other, and immersed in thought, did not say anything for quite a while.

Waiting in tense expectation, Winona barely breathed. She could hardly believe this was happening to her, that her happy existence was being threatened by someone she had rarely spoken to in years. They had been friendly during their childhood, but that had been over 20 years ago and she had been friends with all the boys in the village, not just him.

Jumping Bull cleared his throat. "I want you and I mean to have you. No one will stand in my way." He picked up the haunch. "For now, think on my words and settle in your mind that you are going to be my wife whether you like the idea or not."

"Never!" Winona declared, her eyes flashing. "I would rather . . ." She then fell silent because the object of her wrath had risen and departed.

Suddenly Winona began trembling uncontrollably. Doubling over, she clutched her stomach and uttered a series of low, pathetic groans. Acute misery tore at her soul. Clenching her fists, she craned her neck back and gazed out the opening at the top of the lodge. *Oh my Nate!* her mind cried. *Where are you?*

Rolling Thunder held a hand aloft as he reined up, and the other four also halted. The scent of smoke was strong in his nostrils, and he could hear an unusual thumping sound. They were close to the fire, he knew, so he slid off his war-horse, tied it to a bush, and motioned for the rest to follow him.

Hefting the slender lance in his left hand, Rolling Thunder glided through the undergrowth until he spotted a meadow ahead. There was movement at the far end, so he dropped into a crouch and snaked forward until he had an unobstructed view. His face fairly gleamed with bloodlust when he discovered the source of the fire.

A bearded white man had made camp beside a small spring and was busily chopping wood with an ax. Several packs lay on the ground by the fire, as did a bundle of beaver pelts. To a tree behind him were secured two mules and a horse. Leaning against the tree was a rifle.

Rolling Thunder glanced at his companions and used sign language to convey his directions. Walking Bear and Loud Talker he sent to the left, Bobcat and Little Dog to the right. As they moved away he sank to his hands and knees, then onto his belly, and crawled into the open, moving through the high grass as would a slinking wolf.

When a mere 15 feet from the unsuspecting trapper, Rolling Thunder released his spear and lowered his right hand to his knife. Killing a foe in personal combat rated as a braver act than killing one from a distance, so rather than hurl the lance he intended to get in close and dispatch the man with the keen blade that glinted in the bright sunlight.

Rolling Thunder edged nearer, his eyes exclusively on the white man. The others would hold back, giving him the honor of making the kill. He gripped the knife firmly and closed to within ten feet.

Abruptly, the trapper stopped chopping and looked up sharply, his blue eyes roving over the meadow and the ring of pines. By the anxious glances he shot in all directions it was apparent that he sensed danger but had nothing solid on which to base his apprehension. He lowered the ax, stared at the horse and mules to see if they were agitated, and when he saw them standing placidly, chuckled and resumed chopping.

Coiling his legs under him, Rolling Thunder waited until the man had finished splitting the thick piece of wood and was bending over to pick it up. Then, like a shot, Rolling Thunder charged, his knife held on high for a killing stroke.

The trapper, on hearing onrushing footsteps, whirled. There was no time for him to grab the flintlock under his belt. Clasping the ax at opposite ends, he swept it up and blocked the powerful swing of Rolling Thunder's arm. Backing away to give himself room to maneuver, he reversed his grip and drove the ax head at the Gros Ventre's face.

By the merest fraction Rolling Thunder ducked under the swing and felt a breath of air fan his cheeks. He lunged, striving to bury his knife in the trapper's chest, but the man was quicker, flinging himself to one side and dropping a hand to the flintlock.

Rolling Thunder knew he must not let the trapper draw that gun. Cutting loose with a feral war whoop, he leaped, his arms outstretched, and collided with the man just as the flintlock was yanked free. Together they toppled, Rolling Thunder on top, his legs preventing the man from raising the pistol.

The trapper's eyes showed fear as Rolling Thunder lifted the knife, shrieked with joy, and buried the blade into the man's throat. Gurgling and wheezing, spurting blood on the two of them and the grass, the trapper bucked, vainly trying to toss the Gros Ventre off. Tenaciously, Rolling Thunder clamped his thighs harder and held onto the knife. He could feel the man's movements growing weaker and weaker. A single word escaped the trapper's blood-flecked lips.

"God—!"

Suddenly it was over. The trapper went limp, his eyes blank. Rolling Thunder jerked out the dripping knife and pushed erect. Whooping deliriously, he jumped up and down over and over.

From the trees came his friends. Loud Talker reached the trapper first and struck the body with his tomahawk. "I claim second coup!" he shouted.

"The bastard is dead," Bobcat said. "You cannot claim coup on a dead man."

"I thought I saw him move," Loud Talker objected.

"You wished you saw him move," was Bobcat's retort.

Loud Talker turned to Rolling Thunder. "Was he dead? Do I count coup?"

Rolling Thunder stopped jumping and faced them. He found it hard to think, so furiously was his blood pounding in his veins. Gradually the words sank in, and he looked down at the trapper. According to custom, up to four men could count coup on the same enemy in the heat of battle. The highest coup always went to the warrior who struck an enemy while the enemy was alive, severely wounding him. Second coup would go to another warrior who might then strike the weakened foe. Third coup went to yet a different warrior if he dispatched the wounded adversary, while fourth coup could be claimed by yet another if he did the scalping.

"Do I?" Loud Talker repeated eagerly.

"Yes," Rolling Thunder said, and saw Little Dog frown and turn away. "There was a breath of life left in him when you hit him. The coup counts. I will vouch for you."

"I would have sworn he was dead," Bobcat said, adding instantly, "but you should know better than I, so I will accept your judgment."

Walking Bear was staring enviously at the trapper's

long black hair. He tapped his knife. "Do you want the scalp or may I have it?"

Indecision made Rolling Thunder hesitate. He wanted the scalp badly so that he could gloat to White Buffalo and prove to the rest of the tribe that he could do anything White Buffalo did. But clearly this wasn't the white man they had been after; this wasn't the one who had a boy along, who might or might not be Grizzly Killer. And how much better it would be if he could claim the famous Grizzly Killer's scalp! But if he insisted on having this one, the others would have every right to demand that they be given the chance to count first coup on Grizzly Killer. What should he do? he asked himself. Take a chance on adding Grizzly Killer's hair to his collection and let Walking Bear have this scalp? Or take this one and possibly have to pass up Grizzly Killer's?

As he stood there hesitating, Rolling Thunder noticed Little Dog look at him and smile. Somehow, he knew what his friend was thinking, that he wasn't generous enough to pass up any white man's scalp, no matter how much benefit he might later derive from doing so. Galled, he impulsively stated, "The scalp is yours, Walking Bear."

Turning, Rolling Thunder walked to the tree and claimed the rifle for his own. He also claimed the horse and one of the packs. The rest divided up the spoils as they saw fit. Both Loud Talker and Walking Bear thanked him repeatedly, and to each he was properly humble. He made no mention of the elation he felt at having the two of them in his debt. They were so grateful they would go along with whatever he wanted—and shortly he spoke out. "I would like to try one more time to find the trail of the man and the boy."

"Why go to the bother?" Little Dog said. "They are many miles from here by now."

Tenderfoot

"I want to try."

"You've killed a white man. What more do you need?"

Rolling Thunder made no reply, but the tinge of sadness that touched his face combined with the air of slightly hurt feelings he so cleverly projected had the result he hoped.

Loud Talker promptly came to his defense. "I do not understand why you object to going after them, Little Dog," he declared indignantly. "What harm can it do?" He bobbed his head at Rolling Thunder. "Thanks to him we will be the talk of the village when we return. Why not do as he wants and maybe count more coup?"

"I agree," Walking Bear threw in. "Going back with elk meat is one thing, going back with scalps and many coup to boast of is another. So I say we go after these other two."

Bobcat interjected his predictable opinion. "I would rather kill enemies than elk anytime. Count me in."

Recognizing a lost cause when he saw one, Little Dog walked off. "I will get our horses," he offered so he could be alone with his thoughts. He heard harsh laughter and wondered if he was the source of their humor.

A smoldering anger filled his breast at the way Rolling Thunder was manipulating them. The others were too blinded by bloodlust to see it, but he could. He was of half a mind to desert them and go back alone. Yet he couldn't bring himself to abandon them to their own stupidity no matter what the personal consequences might be. The true mark of genuine friendship, he had long maintained, was that friends stuck together through good times and bad, through periods of peace and happiness and interludes of danger and death. So what sort of person would it make him if he went back without them?

Little Dog went around a tree, still pondering. Since

59

his was the sole voice of reason, it was his responsibility to see that the others didn't put themselves in an unnecessarily perilous situation. He would serve as their guardian spirit for the duration of the hunt, and if in his estimation they wanted to take any pointless risks, he would advise them accordingly. Should they heed him, fine. If not, then at least he would have done all that was required of a true friend.

In due course they were on their way to the river. Rolling Thunder was confident they'd find the trail again if they continued searching both shores. Peeved that Little Dog was still questioning his judgment, Rolling Thunder studiously avoided talking to him until they were both again moving along the bank, their eyes studying the soft earth for telltale spoor.

"Call out if you see anything," he said.

"Do you think I would not?" Little Dog responded.

"I can no longer tell what you will do," Rolling Thunder said gravely. "There was a time when you were the most dependable man I know, but now you are like an old woman whose mind no longer works right. If you persist in disputing every idea I have, I doubt I will take you along the next time I lead a raiding party."

"Whatever you feel is best," Little Dog said coldly, and resolved right then and there to sever his ties with Rolling Thunder once they were among their own kind again. It would serve Rolling Thunder right if he went on a raid with White Buffalo instead, thereby making public his dissatisfaction and showing everyone else which warrior he felt was better suited to be their next chief.

Considerable time had elapsed when Rolling Thunder passed a dense thicket that grew right down to the water's edge. He had been forced to enter the river to swing around it, and as he angled to the shore he happened to glance back. Instantly he wheeled his war-horse and cut loose with piercing whoops in elation. Imprinted in the soil were the familiar tracks he sought. Jumping down, he examined the impressions, grinning at the craftiness of their quarry.

If it was Grizzly Killer, the man knew all the tricks. Plunging into the thicket when he had left the water was a smart move since the tangle of vegetation hid most of the hoofprints.

"But not all of them," Rolling Thunder said softly to himself, and remounted. Walking Bear, Bobcat, and Loud Talker were fording to his side. He waited for them, pointed out the trail, then assumed the lead.

Little Dog brought up the rear. Secretly he had hoped they wouldn't find the tracks again so they could get on with the business of hunting elk. Now, knowing Rolling Thunder as he did, he was certain they would push on until nightfall and resume the pursuit at first light, stopping only for short periods, and then only because their horses needed occasional rest.

Once again, Little Dog noted, the trail was taking them deeper into Shoshone territory, although in a roundabout manner. He speculated that the man they were after must think he had lost them. Soon they came to where the pair had camped.

Rolling Thunder jumped down to press his palm to the charred embers. He was on one knee when the brush to their left rustled loudly and out stepped a squat, stocky animal that bristled at the sight of them and voiced a challenging snarl.

None of them moved. None of them spoke. They did not want to do a thing that would provoke the newcomer into attacking, since despite its relatively small stature the wolverine was one of the most feared creatures in the mountains. It was only three feet long and less than two feet high, but what it lacked in size it more than compensated for by possessing a tenacious, savage disposition unmatched by any other beast or man.

This one was a female, her color a mix of black and brown, her long claws visible as she unexpectedly turned to one side to go around the party. Exhibiting an odd shuffling gait, she took her time, her baleful gaze fixed on them the whole time.

Rolling Thunder was tempted to use his lance. A wolverine pelt was a rare trophy, even more prized than that of a grizzly. But being the only one dismounted, he would be the object of her unstoppable wrath should he hurl his lance into her but fail to drop her on the spot. Prudence made him hold still until she darted into the undergrowth and continued on her undisturbed way.

Just like that the incident, so fraught with the potential for violence, was over. In itself it was not remarkable, since many such incidents occurred in the lifetime of the Gros Ventres. But it gave one of them an opening he tried to exploit.

"That was a bad omen," Little Dog said. "We should turn back."

"It would have been a bad omen had the animal attacked," Rolling Thunder disagreed, rising. "That it did not is proof that our medicine is strong and that soon Grizzly Killer and the young one will be our captives."

Loud Talker grunted assent. "Yes, friend! Our medicine is strong! No one can stand up to us, not Grizzly Killer, not even the entire Shoshone nation. Let us hurry, and maybe by tonight one of us will be the proud owner of a new scalp."

Presently five warriors rode on, but only four of them were smiling in anticipation.

Join the Western Book Club and GET 4 FREE* BOOKS NOW!
A $19.96 VALUE!

Yes! I want to subscribe to the Western Book Club.

Please send me my **4 FREE* BOOKS**. I have enclosed $2.00 for shipping/handling. Each month I'll receive the four newest Leisure Western selections to preview for 10 days. If I decide to keep them, I will pay the Special Members Only discounted price of just $3.36 each, a total of $13.44, plus $2.00 shipping/handling ($19.50 US in Canada). This is a **SAVINGS OF AT LEAST $6.00** off the bookstore price. There is no minimum number of books I must buy, and I may cancel the program at any time. In any case, the **4 FREE* BOOKS** are mine to keep.

*In Canada, add $5.00 shipping/handling per order
for the first shipment. For all future shipments to
Canada, the cost of membership is $16.25 US,
which includes shipping and handling.
(All payments must be made in US dollars.)

NAME: _____

ADDRESS: _____

CITY: _____ STATE: _____

COUNTRY: _____ ZIP: _____

TELEPHONE: _____

E-MAIL: _____

SIGNATURE: _____

If under 18, Parent or Guardian must sign. Terms, prices, and conditions subject to change. Subscription subject to acceptance. Dorchester Publishing reserves the right to reject any order or cancel any subscription.

Chapter Five

Nate King raised his Hawken and trained the barrel on the large four-legged shape that had materialized behind them among the pines. Before he could take deliberate aim, however, the thing was on them. Or rather, going around them. Father and son sat in amused amazement as a ten-point blacktail buck dashed like lightning past their horses and into trees a dozen feet away.

Zachary broke into relieved laughter. "Tarnation, Pa! What caused that critter to act up so?"

"Something must have spooked him a ways back," Nate said. "Sometimes deer will run for miles when they're scared."

"Too bad we didn't shoot it," Zach said. "I'd like some roast venison. Wouldn't you?"

"Perhaps tonight," Nate said, and resumed their interrupted journey. To the southwest reared a large mountain sprinkled with patches of white at the summit—lingering vestiges of last year's snows that had not melted over the summer, and probably wouldn't melt before the first snow of the new winter season struck the Rockies. Some of the mountains were so high that snow stayed on their peaks the year around. They made their way toward this lofty monarch, always mindful to check their back trail now and again for signs of the five Indians.

On the bottom slope they came on a small, oval pond created by runoff from higher up. At one end grew cattails in profusion. Nate indicated the clusters of long, rigid stalks, swordlike leaves, and brown seed heads, then said, "You'll never go hungry with those around."

"Why, Pa?" the boy asked.

"Because there isn't a plant in all creation that fills a man's belly so many ways like a cattail," Nate said, and launched into detail. "In early spring you can peel and eat the stalks. Raw or boiled, they're delicious. In late spring you can cut off the green heads, husk them, and throw them in a pot to boil until they're tender. In early summer the heads are ripe enough to eat raw. Then, from the end of summer on through until the next spring, you can eat the horn-shaped sprouts that grow down at their base."

Zach was duly impressed. "Where did you learn all that?"

"From your mother and other Shoshones," Nate said. "And that's not all. If you mash a cattail flower up, you can use it as a salve for burns and cuts. Never forget too that the leaves give off a sticky juice that kills pain."

"I'll be!" Zach exclaimed, eyeing the growth at the border of the pond with new appreciation. "I could have used some the time I had a toothache."

Nate nodded, and moving Pegasus closer to the cattails, he reached out and tapped a brown head. "These make great tinder for starting a fire." Bending down, he touched a stalk. "And these, in a pinch, make do as an arrow shaft."

"Is there anything a cattail *isn't* good for?" Zach joked.

Once in the pines Nate carried on with his lesson, instructing his son in how to tell the different types of pines apart. All of them, he stressed, had parts a man could eat; the bark itself would keep someone alive indefinitely, a tasty tea could be concocted from a handful of needles if the needles were chopped up into tiny bits and boiled for about five minutes first, and the seeds were as edible for people as they were for squirrels.

Zach paid careful attention. He knew that the skills he was learning now might make the difference between life and death at some later time in his life. Fresh in his fertile mind were the many times he had encountered the dead: free trappers who had succumbed to hunger or hostiles or the elements, warriors slain in warfare or while out hunting, women who had died during enemy raids or who had been torn apart by fierce beasts. Having seen so much death, he was the more determined not to add his own life to the Grim Reaper's toll. The wilderness was no place for greenhorns, as his Uncle Shakespeare had so often said, so Zach wanted to learn all he could. One day, he vowed, he'd be as competent a mountain man as Shakespeare or his father.

So engrossed did Nate become in enlightening his son about the varied bounties lying all around them that he was surprised, on gazing beyond Zach, to discover they had traveled over a mile up the side of the mountain. Facing front, he rode from the trees into a grassy belt separating the pines from the higher aspens, and as he did a tremendous gust of chill air rushed out of the north and fanned him from head to toe.

Startled, Nate stared to the north, and was disturbed to see a few slate-gray clouds floating over the crest of an adjoining peak. If he didn't know better, he told himself, he'd swear there might be snow on the way. But it was too early in the year for a snowstorm. The worst he could expect was a dusting, which worried him not at all. It would not be hard to locate or construct adequate shelter in which the two of them could wait out any cold snap.

So upward they rode, Nate on the constant lookout for elk or sign of elk. In the aspens he slowed and searched diligently, thinking some had possibly bedded down there for the day. Yet it was not until the aspens were a hundred yards below them, when they were riding along the base of a serrated line of huge boulders situated close to the patches of snow at the summit, that Nate finally spied what he had journeyed so far to find.

Three elk stood on a barren spine that split the aspens as a cleaver would meat. One was a bull, the others cows, and all three had their attention riveted on something or other down at the bottom of the mountain. They had not, as yet, heard the horses.

Stopping, Nate beamed at his son and pointed. Zach nodded excitedly. The range, Nate estimated, was close to three hundred yards. To be certain of bringing one down he must get closer, and with that end in mind he dismounted, used sign language to direct Zach to do the same, and led the boy into a ravine that would bring them out very near the unsuspecting elk.

Halfway along, Nate tied both horses to high bushes. His Hawken clutched in two hands, he crept lower and lower until he caught sight of the three animals. They were still staring downward. Motioning for Zach to stay close to him, he worked his way from cover to cover and reached a boulder 70 yards away and 20 yards below the elk.

Quietly resting the Hawken barrel on a boulder, Nate cocked the piece and took a bead on the bull, aiming at a spot just behind its front shoulder. A properly placed ball would either kill it outright or pierce its lungs and so weaken it that the animal would not be able to flee very far. He was all set to squeeze the trigger when an idea occurred to him that brought a gleam to his eyes. "You do it, son," he whispered.

"Me, Pa?" Zach was dubious. "I ain't never shot an animal that big before."

"Then it's time you learned."

"But what if I miss?"

"Every man does, one time or another. Now hurry before they walk off."

Gulping, dismayed at the responsibility suddenly thrust on him, Zach reluctantly stepped to the boulder and rested the tip of the Kentucky's barrel on the upper edge. He had to lift onto the balls of his feet to see clearly the length of the gun. Wedging the stock tight against his shoulder as his father had taught him to do, he sighted on the bull. Then he hesitated. Butterflies swarmed in his stomach and his arms felt unaccountably weak.

"Relax," Nate whispered. "Remember to cock the hammer, and don't touch the trigger until you're ready to fire." He reached out. "I have complete faith in you."

Zach felt his father's hand squeeze his shoulder in encouragement and his nervousness drained from him, to be replaced by a budding confidence in his own ability. His father never lied. If his father trusted him to make the shot and believed he was capable of making it count, then he must be able to do it.

Curling his small thumb around the hammer, Zach pulled back until there was an audible click. He aimed down the barrel, taking his time, wanting to be sure, to make his pa proud of him. The bull took a step, so he slid the barrel a fraction along the boulder to compensate.

Zach recalled everything his father had ever taught him about shooting a rifle. "Hold the barrel steady.

Match up the sights in a straight line to the target. Right before you're about to shoot, hold your breath. Never jerk the trigger. Squeeze it gently."

A booming retort rolled out across the slope and echoed off nearby mountains. All three elk broke into a run, but the bull staggered, took several faltering strides, and collapsed in a whirl of limbs and antlers. Never slowing, the two cows fled into the aspens.

"You did it!" Nate cried happily, and clapped the boy on the back. "I knew you could."

Zach gaped at the prone bull, then at the smoke curling upward from the rifle muzzle. "I did, didn't I? I really and truly did."

"Come on," Nate urged, dashing around the boulder. "The bull might still be alive. You never want to let an animal suffer any more than is necessary."

They chugged up to where the elk lay in a spreading pool of blood. More blood seeped from its nostrils and trickled from the corners of its mouth. The bull's eyes were locked wide and lifeless, its tongue hanging out. No more shots were needed.

"You did right fine," Nate complimented Zach again. "Perforated its lungs. I couldn't have done any better myself."

"My first elk," Zach said, in awe of his accomplishment. Close up, the bull was immense, over five feet high at the shoulders and nearly ten feet long. It had a dark brown mane of sorts under its throat and its legs were much darker than the body. The rump patch and the tail were yellowish-brown. "How much do you reckon this critter weighs, Pa?" he inquired.

"This one?" Nate made some mental calculations. "I'd figure eight hundred pounds or better."

"Eight hundred!" Zach exclaimed. "Why, that's enough meat to last us ten years."

"Not the way you eat."

68

"How will we get it back to the village? We can't pack out that much on our horses."

"We'll rig up a travois, just like the one we use to haul the lodge back and forth to our cabin when we visit the Shoshones."

"You think of everything."

Nate smiled and patted his son on the head. "In the wilderness a man has to. One slip, one little mistake, can cost you your life." He motioned at the ravine. "Now why don't you fetch the horses and I'll start the butchering?"

"Right away," Zach said, whirling. But he had covered only ten feet when his father called his name. Puzzled, he halted and looked back. "Sir?"

"Aren't you forgetting something?"

"What?"

"That Kentucky of yours won't do you much good if you run into a grizzly or a panther."

"Why . . . ?" Zach began, and abruptly knew what his father was getting at. Grinning sheepishly, he set the stock on the ground and grasped his powder horn. "Always reload as soon as you shoot," he said, repeating his father's previous instruction. "Only an idiot goes traipsing off into the woods with an unloaded gun."

"You're learning," Nate said proudly.

The remainder of the afternoon was a busy one. They rolled the bull onto its back, then removed the hide. The first step entailed slitting the elk open down the back of each hind leg and across the middle of its belly to its chin. Slits were also made down the inside of the front legs, from the knee joint to the belly cut. Next the hide was peeled from the body. They had to cut ligaments and muscles which held it to the carcass, and Nate taught Zach how to always keep the edge of the knife slanted toward the carcass and away from the hide to keep from cutting it.

Nate had planned to rig up a travois and take the carcass down into the trees where they would dry strips of meat over a low fire, but the weather dictated differently. Within an hour after Zach had shot the bull the temperature had dropped some 30 degrees and kept on dropping. The azure sky was transformed into a gray slate with low, ominous clouds stretching from horizon to horizon. They could see their breath when they breathed, and the tips of their fingers were becoming numb with cold.

Zach stuck his hands under his arms and hopped up and down. "I'm about froze, Pa. Is it going to snow?"

"Looks that way," Nate said, casting an apprehensive glance at the threatening heavens. He'd lived through enough winters in the Rockies to know the makings of a first-rate storm when he saw one. Every indication was there: the plummeting temperature, the northerly wind, the moisture-laden clouds. But he kept telling himself that there wouldn't be much snowfall because it was too early in the year.

Just as they finished cutting off the hide and set to the messy work of butchering the meat, the first flakes fell. A few initially, great, flowery flakes that resembled flower petals floating through the air. They landed here, there, and all around the father and son, growing in number with surprising swiftness until within the short span of several minutes the air swarmed as with a multitude of silent white bees.

Nate stopped carving and glanced skyward. Flakes plastered his face, getting into his eyes. He wiped the back of his sleeve across them and straightened. Already the snow was so thick that he could barely distinguish the horses, standing not quite ten feet off. The wind picked up, blowing against his back so strongly it sent the whangs on his buckskins to flapping crazily.

"Pa," Zach commented, "I think we're in for a blizzard."

70

"It won't be that bad," Nate assured him, although he didn't feel quite as confident as he sounded. Suddenly an eerie howling erupted from on high, caused by the wind shrieking past the high peaks and jagged pinnacles. Mary, the mare, frightened by the din, whinnied in fright. As if to accent her fear, the snow increased.

"What'll we do, Pa?" Zach asked nervously.

Nate was debating their options. The meat would keep for days if the temperature stayed low enough. Already the carcass had started to freeze, rendering the butchering job extremely difficult and making it next to impossible to complete the chore in under an hour to an hour and a half. By then they would be half-frozen themselves and the horses would be suffering terribly. Shelter was their first priority; a fire their second.

Which way should they go? Nate wondered. He gazed down the mountain, but could see no further than a few yards. Finding somewhere down below to take cover in the driving storm would be next to impossible. Fortunately, he knew of one place, a spot they'd passed earlier, higher up. Squaring his shoulders, he jammed his knife into its beaded sheath, rolled up the hide, picked up the Hawken, and stepped to Zach's side. "We're going up to those boulders near the summit. Whatever you do, don't stray off."

"I understand."

Nate took his son's left hand and hurried toward the horses. To his consternation, he couldn't see either one. The swirling snow formed an impenetrable white shroud. Pausing, he focused on where he thought they should be, and walked on until he nearly bumped into Pegasus. Then he quickly gave Zach a boost onto the mare.

After tying the hide on behind the saddle, Nate climbed into the stirrups, and was set to start off when a chilling thought prompted him to reach into a parfleche hanging just in back of his right leg and take out a length of rawhide rope he always toted. One end of the rope he tied to his saddle, the other to Zach's saddle. "This way," he explained as he made the knots fast, "we won't get separated."

"You might not ever find me again if we did," Zach said, grinning. He was cold to the bone, but not overly worried since his father appeared to be taking the advent of the storm so calmly. Positive his pa would take care of him, he tucked his chin in and listened to the howling wind.

Nate took the lead and gingerly picked his way down the slope toward the ravine, relying on his finely honed sense of direction since the whipping snow obscured every landmark. Once, years ago, when he was still a greenhorn, he would have been hopelessly lost had he been caught in a driving snowstorm. Now, thanks to the countless miles he'd spent crisscrossing the mountains in search of beaver, he'd developed an innate sense for telling which way was which, almost as if an internal compass guided him. Many Indians shared the same knack.

Several times over the years, in inclement weather, he'd been compelled to rely on his instincts when there had been no other means of determining the right direction to proceed, but never had he been caught in anything so elementally fierce as the raging storm that enveloped them. It had gotten so bad he could barely see his hand in front of his face, so he relied on other factors such as the slant of his horse to confirm when they came to the bottom of the spine and were on level ground again. Turning to the right, he carefully picked his way, watchful for boulders and other obstacles that were often no more than indistinct dark shapes against the background of the falling snow. By exercising unflagging attention he was able to avoid them.

Advancing at a snail's pace was the only way to be safe, but Nate chafed at the delay. He wanted to get his son under cover rapidly, and he knew just the spot. As they'd been riding along the base of the huge boulders a couple of hours ago, they'd passed a wide crack in the ground between two of the monoliths. Covered by a dome of earth, the opening would be an excellent shelter in which to wait out Nature's fury.

First, though, Nate had to find it. An eternity dragged by as he picked his path up the ravine. Once Pegasus, despite his best efforts, blundered into a boulder, but was not seriously hurt. Eventually, when his teeth were close to chattering and his body felt like it was covered with gooseflesh, Nate became sure they had emerged from the ravine, and guessed the boulders lay ahead and to his left.

Nate bore onward toward his goal. An inch of snow covered the ground, and he tried not to think of what would happen should the gelding slip and fall. He and Zach would both go down. He dreaded the idea of one of them sustaining a broken neck or some other horrible injury, and redoubled his concentration so as not to invite a mishap.

Another eternity went by. Nate began to think he'd made a mistake after all, and that somehow he had missed the long row of rocky sentinels. Then, looming black and stark in front of him, one of them appeared. Instantly another problem presented itself. He had no way of knowing if he was north of the cleft or south of it. If he picked the wrong direction, they might never find it, and vermin would be gnawing at their bones come the spring.

Briefly Nate hesitated. Mary had halted next to Pegasus, and one look at his freezing son, hunched low against the biting wind, covered thick with snow, was enough to goad him into action. Forming a silent prayer for deliverance, he turned southward and hugged the base of the boulders.

Here the wind was not quite as strong, the snow not quite as heavy. Still, his range of vision was restricted to ten feet straight ahead. The gelding walked briskly, as eager as he was to get out of the storm. And shortly, as welcome a sight as an oasis to a wandering soul in a blistering desert, the cleft materialized on his right.

Nate drew rein and slid to the ground, his legs stiff, his body devoid of all warmth. The opening was wider than he had remembered, twice the width of a horse. Poking his head in, he found the interior to be as spacious as his single-room cabin and close to eight feet high.

Delighted, Nate lost no time in leading both horses within. Mary balked, and had to be persuaded with a cuff and a sharp tug before she would enter. In a single step he reached Zach, and tenderly lifted the boy to the dirt floor. "Let me help you," he said as he did.

"I'm about plumb frozen," Zach mustered manfully, and smiled. "The next time we go elk hunting, can we do it in the summer?"

Nate's laugh was longer and louder than it needed to be, but his son apparently didn't notice. Gazing about, Nate was overjoyed to find that someone—Indians, most likely—had sheltered here once before. Near a back corner lay the charred remains of a fire, and beside it were a dozen or so branches that had been gathered but not used. In addition, a number of weeds had taken root near the entrance, and although they were now brown and withered, they were dry and would burn readily.

Working swiftly, Nate pulled out handfuls of the weeds and hurried to the corner. Making a circular bed of the weeds, he properly arranged some of the branches on top, using the limbs sparingly, acutely aware the limited supply might have to last them quite a while.

From his possibles bag he took his flint and steel and tinderbox. Bending down, he prepared a small bed of punk, which consisted of dry, decayed maple wood he had collected over the summer. Next he proceeded to strike the steel against the flint to cause showers of sparks to fall on the tinder. Once he saw it catch, he carefully fanned the infant flames with his breath, nursing them to life.

"You're doing it, Pa!" Zach cried at his side.

The tinder caught, the flames grew, and Nate added bits of dry weed, feeding the hungry fire. Presently one of the branches also burst into flames, and soon light and spreading warmth filled the cleft.

"I never saw a fire look so good," Zach said.

"Me neither," Nate agreed, and cast a glance filled with misgivings at the opening. Outside, the wind continued to wail, the snow continued to fall. The full magnitude of their predicament hit him, and he realized with a start that his son had been right. This was no ordinary snowstorm. It was a full-fledged blizzard.

Chapter Six

The giant pounded his chest with a brawny fist and angrily declared, "There is an easy solution to the problem. I will challenge Jumping Bull, and when we fight I will cut out his heart and feed it to my dogs."

A period of silence ensued as everyone in the lodge exchanged glances. Winona looked at their host, her uncle Spotted Bull, who had called together their immediate relatives and closest friends so the grave situation facing them could be discussed at length and a course of action decided upon. A venerable warrior who had lived over 50 winters, Spotted Bull was not one to let raw emotion eclipse his seasoned wisdom.

"It is all well and good to talk of killing the fool, my son," he now said, resting his hand on the shoulder of the giant. "Many of us would like to do the same. But we must be discreet. This affair must be handled delicately."

Touch the Clouds snorted. "Was Jumping Bull discreet when he brazenly demanded that Winona leave Grizzly Killer and go live with him? Was he discreet when he went out and told everyone what he had done and bragged of how he would humiliate Grizzly Killer if Grizzly Killer objected?" He paused, then answered his own question. "No, he was not! He has not only insulted Grizzly Killer and Winona, he has also insulted all of us who call them our friends. I say let me kill him and be done with it."

Winona scanned the faces of those present, gauging their feelings. Beside her sat Willow Woman, her cousin, whose worry was evident. On her other side was Spotted Bull's wife, Morning Dove, her features grave. And the majority of the men were equally somber. Besides Spotted Bull and Touch the Clouds, there were Lame Elk, one of the oldest men in the tribe, and younger warriors: Drags the Rope, He Who Rides Standing, Paints His Ears Red, and others.

It was Lame Elk who spoke next, and everyone gave him their attention. "It is rare that one man tries to take the wife of another," he mentioned. "In all the time I have lived, I have only seen this happen once before, and that was when Raven Wing tried to take Nape of the Neck's woman. There was much blood shed, and in the end the woman wanted nothing to do with either of them and went to live with someone else."

"I will never leave Grizzly Killer," Winona boldly stated. Normally at such councils the men did all the talking. A woman never volunteered anything unless specifically asked to do so. But she could not sit there and say nothing when her entire future was at stake.

"We all know that," Lame Elk said, bestowing a smile on her. "Not one of us here doubts your love for him or his love for you. But your love is not the issue. The issue is what we must do about Jumping Bull's unwanted advances."

"Grizzly Killer will be back soon," remarked Drags the Rope, who had been Nate's friend longer than any of the others, "and then none of us will have to do a thing. He will put Jumping Bull in his place."

"Until then we must protect Winona," Spotted Bull said. "Jumping Bull might become impatient and try to drag her off against her will. He has a violent temper. We all know how he used to beat his first wife."

"Maybe he will change his mind and nothing will come of this," Paints His Ears Red, the youngest warrior present, remarked.

"Jumping Bull is not one to turn back from something he has started," Spotted Bull said.

Lame Elk leaned forward. "There is more involved here than his interest in Winona, which might be genuine, although I have my doubts."

"What do you mean?" Touch the Clouds interjected.

"Has it not struck any of you as strange that Jumping Bull has shown no interest in Winona before?" Lame Elk said. "And if he wants a new wife so badly, why pick a woman who has pledged herself to someone else? There are many unmarried women who would be happy to share his lodge."

"So?" Touch the Clouds prompted.

"Think about it," said Lame Elk. "How many times have you heard Jumping Bull say that it is a mistake to be friendly with the whites? How many times has he spoken in councils and urged our people to fight the whites and drive them from our land?"

"Many times," said Spotted Bull.

"He hates all whites with a blinding hatred," Lame Elk said. "And he is not alone. There are a few others who share his sentiments. They have never treated Grizzly Killer as one of us and never will. Some of them have gone so far as to say in council that we should turn our backs on him and not allow him to live with us now and again as we do."

No one said anything for a while. Winona, along with the rest, was deep in thought, contemplating the implications of the old warrior's statements. Fresh in her mind were Jumping Bull's words: "A white man is no fit husband for a beautiful woman like you."

Spotted Bull voiced the thoughts they all shared. "So the real reason behind Jumping Bull's despicable conduct is that he wants to provoke Grizzly Killer into a fight and kill him."

"Such would be my guess," Lame Elk said. "He may truly desire Winona, but he is using his desire to justify his hatred. He hopes that when Grizzly Killer returns and learns that he has been courting Winona, Grizzly Killer will go after him. Which Grizzly Killer will. Then Jumping Bull can kill him and claim he had to do it in self-defense."

"The bastard!" Touch the Clouds said. "We should report this to the Yellow Noses."

The suggestion sparked hope in Winona's breast. Like many another tribe, the Shoshones boasted certain special societies for both men and women, among them the Yellow Noses, an elite group including only the bravest of warriors. Among their many functions was the policing of the village and the maintaining of order when the Shoshones were on the march. If disputes arose, the Yellow Noses settled them, and their decisions were final. Any warrior who opposed them was liable to be beaten, perhaps have his weapons confiscated or broken, or have his lodge cut to pieces. They had the authority to tell Jumping Bull to leave Nate and her alone, which would end the whole matter. But the next moment Winona's hope was dashed by Lame Elk.

"No, we cannot go to the Yellow Noses. I will tell you why." His craggy features were downcast. "The Yellow Noses can only act when tribal rules have been broken, such as when a man goes off and hunts alone even though the word has been given that we will make a surround. And this is as it should be, for a man who does that might scare off all the game and leave the rest of the village hungry." He sighed and gazed sadly at Winona. "But there is no rule against one man taking another's wife if he can convince the woman to go with him. So long as he does not assault her husband, he does nothing wrong."

"So you are saying we must sit back and do nothing?" Touch the Clouds inquired in disgust.

"Our people have always been free to do as they want so long as they do not harm others," Lame Elk said. "This is as it should be."

"So we do *nothing*?" Touch the Clouds said harshly.

"I am afraid so," Lame Elk said. "Unless Jumping Bull harms Winona, we are powerless. Grizzly Killer must deal with this himself when he gets back."

Touch the Clouds looked at Spotted Bull. "And you, Father? What do you say?"

"I am sorry. I must agree with Lame Elk."

Winona averted her face so none could see the sorrow and disappointment reflected in her eyes. Accustomed as she was to handling her problems herself, it had been hard for her to confide in her cousin, Willow Woman, and even harder to agree to a council after Willow Woman had gone and informed her father, Spotted Bull.

"Do not fear, Winona," Spotted Bull now said. "We will make it known that Jumping Bull must answer to us if he lays a hand on you before your husband returns. He will not dare bother you."

*   *   *

Twilight covered the village as, a short while later, Winona made her slow way toward her lodge, her heart heavy at the outcome of the meeting. Despite the sympathy and the promises her relatives and friends had voiced, she knew that she was on her own. It had been foolish, she reflected, to expect them to resolve the situation for her. They had their own lives to live. A grown woman had no business running to others when trouble presented itself. What would Nate think of her behavior?

Ironically, it was on his behalf that Winona had swallowed her pride and done the unthinkable. She knew her husband's temperament, knew he would tear into Jumping Bull the moment he heard what had transpired. Neither of them would give any quarter; one or the other would die. And while she had complete confidence in Nate's prowess, she had heard about too many outstanding fighters who had been killed by unworthy adversaries not to worry about him. All it would take was a single misstep or a fleeting instant of distraction and Nate might be slain.

Suddenly her pondering came to an end. A shadow had detached itself from between two nearby lodges and fallen into step at her elbow. "I would walk with you," Jumping Bull said.

"Go walk off a cliff," Winona responded bitterly, slanting to the left so their arms would not brush together.

"I have important words to say."

"Tell them to a tree."

"You will listen," Jumping Bull declared, and seized hold of her wrist.

Red rage transformed Winona into a furious she-wolf. She whirled, yanking her wrist free, and snarled spitefully, "Don't touch me! Don't *ever* touch me."

81

David Thompson

Something in her tone made Jumping Bull take a step backward. He saw her hatred, saw her fingers clenched like claws, and for a moment he believed she was about to spring on him. Instinctively he went to raise an arm to strike her across the face and put her in her place. Then, awakening to the gravity of the error he was about to commit, he let the arm drop. She was not his *yet*.

"If you ever lay a hand on me again I will not wait for my husband to slay you," she said. "I will do it myself."

"Calm down so we can talk without arguing," Jumping Bull coaxed.

"Do not waste your breath," Winona responded. Pivoting, she stalked off. She was so mad she trembled. Her right hand touched the knife on her hip and she closed her fingers on the hilt.

"Very well," Jumping Bull said. "If you do not want to hear how bloodshed can be avoided, do as you please."

Winona stopped, her curiosity contending with her loathing of the vile animal who presumed to try and steal her affections from the man she loved. Reluctantly, suspecting she was somehow playing into Jumping Bull's hands, she turned. "Explain."

"I thought you might like to have the white dog's life spared and I have a way it can be done."

"Try talking with a straight tongue for once."

The corners of the husky warrior's mouth curved upward. "If you will agree to come with me, right this moment, I will let your husband live."

"What game is this you are playing?" Winona snapped. "You already know how I feel. But since you seem to have your ears plugged with wax, I will tell you again so there will be no mistake." Lightning danced in her eyes. "I will never, ever live with you. I would rather open my wrists first. And from now until my husband comes back, I will keep a loaded pistol at

82

my side. If you dare bother me again, I will use it."

Rolling Thunder's features clouded. Everyone in the village knew her white bastard of a husband had taught her how to use the weapons of the whites, and it was said she could hit a mark 20 yards away dead center ten times out of ten. He moved toward her, his muscular arms tensing. "Then I shall see to it that you never reach your pistol. I will take you with me now."

"Try!" Winona cried, the single word a ringing challenge.

"Yes," spoke a deep voice from the darkness. "Why not try, Jumping Bull, and see what happens next?"

In a blur, Jumping Bull spun, his right hand dropping to the tomahawk at his waist, a malevolent scowl twisting his countenance. "You!" he blurted.

"Yes, me," Touch the Clouds declared as he strolled forward to stand next to Winona. So huge was he that next to him she seemed a little girl by comparison. "I heard the words you spoke."

"What of them?" Jumping Bull snapped, prudently easing his hand from the tomahawk. He was no fool. The weapon would make no difference at all in a clash between them; he stood absolutely no chance against the giant. With his own eyes he had once witnessed a fight between Touch the Clouds and three Sioux in which the giant had slain them without working up a sweat. Another time he had seen Touch the Clouds, armed with just a war club, slay a panther half the size of a bear. Only someone with a death wish would confront the giant alone.

"You can thank your guardian spirit that my father has made me give my word that I will not kill you before Grizzly Killer returns," Touch the Clouds stated sternly, "or you would now be lying in a puddle of your own blood."

Jumping Bull glanced toward Spotted Bull's lodge. "Your father made you make such a promise?" he asked in scarcely concealed delight.

"Regrettably, yes." Touch the Clouds rested a hand on Winona's shoulder. "But if you persist in molesting this dear woman, who is like a sister to me, I will be strongly tempted to do something I have never done before. I just might break my promise and gut you like the cur you are."

A hot retort was on Jumping Bull's lips, but he held his temper in check. This development, he reflected, was too good to be believed. His main worry had been that friends of King's would interfere with his plan, and of them all Touch the Clouds was the one to fear the most. But not any more.

It was obvious the giant was restraining himself with an effort. His enormous fists clenched and unclenched as he said, "My father and others are of the opinion that this is a matter strictly between Grizzly Killer and you. Against my better judgment, I have gone along with them." His voice lowered. "But heed my words, Jumping Bull. I will not stand by and let you have your way with Winona. She is Grizzly Killer's woman, not yours, and knowing her as I do, I know she will be his until the day he dies."

"Which may not be far off," Jumping Bull could not resist saying. Drawing himself to his full height, he gestured at Winona and said, "But let us not argue over a matter that does not, as your wise father has decided, concern you. I would honor Winona by taking her into my lodge. For the time being, her misguided loyalty to someone who does not deserve her love has clouded her thinking. I am confident, though, she will come around to my way of thinking eventually. And when she does, and she is my wife, I hope the two of us can be friends."

Winona had listened to all she was going to. Turning to Touch the Clouds, she asked, "Would you do me the favor of walking me to my lodge?"

"Gladly," the giant rumbled.

Side by side they moved off. Behind them a mocking laugh came on the chill breeze.

A shiver rippled down Winona's spine, but whether from the cold or her reaction to Jumping Bull's arrogance, she could not say. Then she realized she could see her breath, and pausing, she gazed to the northwest. A vast bank of ugly gray clouds were roiling their frenzied way toward the valley in which the encampment lay.

"We are in for some snow," Touch the Clouds noted absently.

Winona was thinking of her husband and her son. What if they had been caught in a storm? She reminded herself that Nate's woodcraft was the equal of any Shoshone's, that he knew how to survive in the very worst weather. Still, as she well knew, there were always many things that could go wrong. A flickering wave of anxiety washed over her and she pressed a hand to her bosom.

Touch the Clouds, misunderstanding, remarked, "You need not fear Jumping Bull for now. He will not do anything until after Grizzly Killer comes back."

"I hope not," Winona said, continuing toward her lodge.

"If you want, I will keep watch over you until then."

"Think of the talk!" Winona replied, trying to be lighthearted. "Every gossip in the village would wear out her tongue telling about it. And I do not think your wife would like that very much."

"My wife knows I would never dishonor her," the giant said rather defensively.

"As do I," Winona acknowledged, touching his arm. "We have been friends since childhood, and I know there is nothing you would not do for me. But I cannot allow you to put yourself in such a position."

"I do not mind."

"No, Touch the Clouds. My husband would think less of me as a woman if he were to hear that I needed you to fight my battles in his absence. Grizzly Killer is my defender, and if anyone is to put Jumping Bull in his place, it is he."

"Very well. But I will still be around if you need me." Touch the Clouds glanced over his shoulder, insuring they had not been followed. "And I swear that if Jumping Bull lays a hand on you, I will send him on to meet his ancestors."

Her lodge reared before them. Winona stood next to the flap and smiled. "Thank you for escorting me. When Grizzly Killer hears of your concern, he will be very grateful."

"I wish there were more I could do," the giant said. "In my heart I feel that my father and Lame Elk are wrong, but my head says I must do as they want."

"You are the best of friends," Winona assured him. Stooping, she swung the flap wide and entered. The interior was dimly lit by the glowing coals of her fire, which she promptly stoked. The last of her meager supply of limbs had to be used to rekindle the flames, and she knew she would need more long before morning. With snow on the way, the night promised to be extremely cold.

Donning a buffalo-hide robe, Winona walked outside and headed for the bank of the river where cottonwoods grew in profusion. There she moved among the trunks, collecting downed limbs as she went.

Ahead of the oncoming storm raced brisk northerly winds that rustled the brown leaves overhead and bent the more slender trees. Occasionally the wind howled as if alive. In the village horses were neighing, dogs barking, children yelling. The noise was such that Winona could not hear her own footsteps, let alone anyone else's.

The search carried her near the swirling water. As she bent over to pick up a slender branch, her gaze drifted toward the lodges and she saw something or someone move in the undergrowth between her and the village. Freezing, she stared at the vague shape and wondered if it was a person or an animal.

A possible answer occurred to her, causing a gasp to escape her lips. Jumping Bull might have seen her leave her lodge, then followed her! And in her haste to gather wood she had left her pistol behind! Slowly she lowered her knees to the ground and set the branches quietly down. Should Jumping Bull attack, she wanted her hands free to defend herself.

Winona reached under her heavy robe and drew her knife. The shape was moving again, advancing toward the river, and would pass within ten feet of her position, on her left. She could not make out many details, but she saw enough to convince her it definitely was a man and not a beast.

Crouching low, Winona clasped the knife close to her chest. She must make the first strike count. A skilled warrior like Jumping Bull would not give her a second chance, so she must go for his throat or his heart. Her own heart was thudding wildly, and to her dismay her hands started to shake. Gritting her teeth, she steeled her will to the deed she must do.

Suddenly the figure changed course, moving directly toward her.

Winona waited for him to step from the bushes, and then, with a low cry of defiance, she sprang.

Chapter Seven

Rolling Thunder, greatest of Gros Ventres warriors and next in line—in his own mind if not in the minds of all his people—to be the next war chief of the tribe, was in the foulest of moods, as foul as the raging blizzard that had unexpectedly stranded the members of his hunting party deep in Shoshone territory. He stood in the midst of wildly waving aspens and mentally cursed the spirits for placing him in such damnable straits.

His anger was fueled by the knowledge that they had been very close to the man and the boy when the snowstorm hit. He'd pushed the others hard prior to the change in the weather, so hard they had gained a lot of ground on the unsuspecting pair. In his opinion the two would have been in his clutches before the sun set.

And now? Rolling Thunder glared skyward and wished he was a medicine man that he might use his power to make the snow stop. If it kept falling at the current rate, by morning there would be five feet or more covering the mountain. High, high above, the wind shrieked past the peaks, the siren scream matching his disposition perfectly.

The sound of wood being chopped fell on Rolling Thunder's ears, and he turned back to the crude but serviceable conical forts his companions were constructing. There were three such shelters, much like those frequently used by the Blackfeet and their allies. Since they had been caught in the aspens and unable to find a convenient cave or other sanctuary, they were making do as resourcefully as they knew how.

In the middle of the forts blazed a fire protected on two sides by lean-tos. When one of the warriors grew cold, as one often did, he would warm himself by the fire for a while, and then resume chopping and aligning the slender saplings used in the building of their forts. Right now it was Little Dog's turn to rest, and as Rolling Thunder squatted across from him, he glanced up.

"Do not say a word," Rolling Thunder warned.

"I was not planning to."

"No? You do not have to. I know what you are thinking. You blame me for this. If I had not insisted on trailing the man and the boy, we would be on our way back to our own country instead of huddled here in these trees. The storm might have missed us."

"No harm has been done. We can go home when the storm ends."

"Which should make you very happy," Rolling Thunder spat. "You never wanted us to come this far." He pulled his robe tighter around his broad shoulders, and when he spoke next his tone had softened. "Perhaps I should have listened to you, old friend. I do not relish the thought of being stranded here for several sleeps."

"Maybe it will be less."

Rolling Thunder made a sound reminiscent of a bull buffalo about to charge. "Listen to that wind! Look at how heavy the snow falls! This is a blizzard, and we will be lucky if we are not snowed in for an entire moon."

"What does a delay matter? You have your new horse and rifle to take back, and you can tell everyone of the coup you counted on a white man. I would say the hunting trip has been the success you hoped it would be."

"It would have been more of a success if we had caught Grizzly Killer."

"If it is him we were after."

"It is," Rolling Thunder declared.

"How do you know?"

"I feel it deep inside."

Little Dog, saying nothing, selected a broken branch from the pile at his side and fed it to the leaping flames. While he dared not admit to it, he was profoundly thankful the blizzard had obliterated every last trace of the tracks they had been dogging, forcing them to abandon the chase. Further incursions into Shoshone territory would be pointless. Thanks to the snow, they all stood to reach their village with their scalps intact. Had he been alone he would have laughed with relief.

"Why are you smiling?"

Taken aback, Little Dog cupped his hands to his mouth and breathed on his fingers to warm them. He was stalling so he could come up with a suitable answer. "I was thinking of my wife and how happy I will be to see her again."

"You always have been too sentimental," Rolling Thunder said. "I have three wives, and I would rather be out here than stuck in a smoky lodge with any one of them. Their unending chatter is enough to give any man a headache, and their constant nagging makes me want to throw them all off a cliff."

"Why insult them so when you know you love them?"

"Do I?"

There was such heartfelt sincerity in the question that Little Dog looked around sharply. He had long held the opinion that the only person Rolling Thunder truly loved was Rolling Thunder. Tactfully, he had never voiced his belief. And he was quite shocked to have his friend practically admit as much.

"Sometimes I wonder," Rolling Thunder said.

"We all have times where we wish our wives would be eaten by wolves," Little Dog commented. "They probably feel the same way about us."

"Do you really think so?" Rolling Thunder said, his brow creased. "Possibly the wives of other men do, but mine are too content and grateful at having me for their husband to ever speak or think ill of me."

"What man truly knows what goes on in a woman's mind?" Little Dog said.

At that juncture Walking Bear joined them and held his hands out to the fire. "If you two are done warming your bottoms, there is still work to be done. One of the forts is not yet complete."

Little Dog, sighing in resignation since he knew how much Rolling Thunder despised doing menial work, put his palms on the frigid ground and began to push upright. But Rolling Thunder restrained him by pressing on his shoulder.

"You rest, my friend. I will help finish."

"I must do my share of the work," Little Dog protested.

"You have already done more than your share and I have not."

Mystified, Little Dog watched Rolling Thunder walk off. How, he wondered, could someone be so selfish and rude one moment and so considerate and polite the next? Rolling Thunder was a bundle of contradictions, as complicated a man to get to know as Little Dog had ever encountered. There were instances when he wanted

91

to embrace him in friendship; at others he wanted to wring Rolling Thunder's neck.

Life was so strange sometimes.

"Let that old blizzard go on forever!" Zach declared contentedly, shifting his feet so they were closer to the fire, so close his moccasins were in danger of bursting into flames. "We're snug and warm in here."

"For now," Nate agreed, gazing anxiously at the constantly shifting white shroud blanketing the landscape outside of their refuge. "If the snow goes on forever, I'm afraid we'll never dig ourselves out."

"It won't," Zach said, laughing. "I wasn't serious, Pa."

Nate touched his son's knees. "Pull your feet back a bit or you'll be going barefoot when we leave."

The boy complied, and bit off a large piece of jerky.

"Go easy there. We don't know how long our supply of food has to last us."

"Sorry," Zach said, and replaced the portion he had not touched in the beaded parfleche on the earthen floor to his left. He was embarrassed that he had been making a pig of himself, and figured it would be best to talk about something else. "How long do you reckon the wood will hold out?"

"A few more hours yet."

"Then what will we do?" Zach asked, thinking of the bitter cold he'd experienced before his father got the fire going. He'd been as close to being frozen stiff as he ever wanted to be, and he dreaded having to go through the ordeal again.

"I'll go down to the trees and fetch more," Nate said.

"In this?" Zach saw puffs of snow blown into the cleft by the squalling wind. Fleeting panic assailed him as he imagined the sheer horror of being left alone should calamity befall his pa. "How will you find your way back?"

"Simple, son," Nate said, pointing at their piled supplies in the corner. "I'll tie one end of my rope in here, to my saddle, and the other end around my waist, then go down the slope, feeling my ways along, until I find fallen branches or a tree I can chop limbs off of."

"But what if the rope isn't long enough?"

"We have two blankets I can cut into strips to add to it if need be."

"But what if the rope or strips break or become untied?"

Their eyes met. Nate gave his son a light tap on the point of his chin and stated, "It has to be done. There's no way around it. We won't last a day without a fire."

"I wish the snow would stop."

"A minute ago you didn't much care if it snows forever."

"I changed my mind."

Smiling, Nate leaned his back against the wall. The warmth and security made him drowsy and he wearily closed his eyes, wishing he could sleep the clock around. Sleep, however, was a luxury he could ill afford until the weather broke and the cold abated. One of them had to keep the fire going at all times, and Zach was hardly old enough to be entrusted with so important a responsibility.

"Pa!"

Nate's eyes shot open and he straightened, his right hand gripping a pistol. His son was staring at the entrance, but a glance showed Nate only thick snow. "What's the matter?"

"I saw something."

"What?"

"I'm not sure, Pa. An animal of some kind. It poked its head in, spotted us, and backed right out again."

Had Zach imagined seeing something? Nate couldn't help but ask himself as he rose and moved cautiously to the opening. The boy was wound as tight as a fiddle, and Nate knew how a bad case of nerves could play havoc with a person's mind. He'd checked the cleft floor shortly after starting the fire, and except for a few chipmunk tracks had found no evidence of previous inhabitants. Peering out proved pointless; visibility was now restricted to a foot or two, at best. A blast of wind lashed snow in his face, driving him inside.

"See anything?"

"No."

"I saw something, Pa. I really did."

Nate studied the ground bordering the opening, which was covered by three inches of snow, but there were no prints. The wind might have wiped them out, if there had been any there to begin with. He walked back to the fire. "I might as well fetch that wood now as wait until later. The storm doesn't look like it will let up before Christmas."

Zachary stood and visibly composed his features. "Right this minute, you mean?"

"No sense in letting grass grow under us," Nate quipped, yet the boy's somber mood was unaffected. Taking the rawhide rope, he carried his saddle to within a foot of the opening and looped the end of the rope around it.

"What about cutting up our blankets?" Zach asked.

"Only as a last resort," Nate said. He yanked on the rope, testing the knot. "Keep your piece charged and your eyes peeled while I'm gone."

"Shoot sharp's the word," Zach said, stepping to the saddle.

Nodding, Nate made fast the rawhide to his waist,

checked his pistols to verify they were still snug under his belt, and slowly edged outward.

"If you need me, Pa, tug on the rope."

"I will," Nate replied, amused at the notion of Zach coming to his rescue should he find himself in trouble. One so tender in years quite understandably lacked a mature appreciation of the severe dangers that might befall any wanderer in the wilderness at any time.

A tremendous gust of wind punctuated Nate's reverie by nearly bowling him over as he moved into the open. Whirling flakes flitted all around him, and he was encased from head to toe in a fine layer of white. Seizing the rope firmly in his left hand, he tucked his chin low and barreled his way down the slope, battling the wind every foot of the way. His body was buffeted mercilessly; at times he felt as if he was being hammered by invisible fists.

And the cold! Now that Nate was away from the warming influence of the fire, the cold sliced into him like a knife made of ice. In seconds he was freezing, his teeth chattering. He might as well have been naked for all the good his buckskins and buffalo robe were doing him.

Somewhere below was the wood they needed. Hunching forward, Nate dug in his feet and made slow but determined progress. Several times he slipped, but each time his grip on the rope enabled him to stay erect. Twice his moccasins banged against rocks. His right ankle started throbbing.

When Nate guessed he had covered 20 feet, he crouched and felt the ground in front of him with his right hand, seeking the precious wood they needed to survive. His frantic fingers found stones by the bushel, rocks by the score, and a few boulders here and there. He also found weeds and a patch of grass. Yet no branches, not so much as a solitary twig.

His fingers were rapidly numbing. Intense pangs racked his lungs. Suddenly his beaver hat began to slip from his head and he pulled it down tight. In doing so he lost his hold on the rope, and as he swung his arm to grab it his left heel went out from under him. Unable to keep his balance, he fell hard.

For a moment Nate lay there, annoyed at his clumsiness. A snowflake landed in his open mouth, alighting on the very tip of his tongue. Instantly it melted and he swallowed the drop of water. There were so many flakes filling the air that another immediately flew between his lips and he swallowed again. "We won't want for water," he said aloud, and chuckled, envisioning how he must look lying there like some simpleton.

Slowly Nate rose, gathering in the rope as he did. "You're not beating us, storm," he declared, then shouted into the raging elements, "You're not beating us!"

Pressing on, Nate searched faster. Visibility had dropped to less than six inches. His arms and legs were so cold they hardly had any feeling left in them. His toes were either numb or missing. The norther was the culprit. High winds invariably intensified cold temperatures.

Desperation tinged his movements now. They needed wood, and he refused to go back to the cleft until he found some. Swinging right and left, he tried to make sense of the objects his fingers touched. A moment later his right hand brushed against something long and hard. Pausing, he examined it carefully and recognized the smooth texture of bark. His prize was a downed tree limb!

Quickly, Nate seized it under his right arm and stood. As he turned a dark blur moved through the snow. He caught a brief glimpse of something on four legs, and knew his son had indeed seen an animal. But what kind?

Nate warily headed for the cleft. Whatever the thing was, it must have followed him down. Would it attack? Or was it as cold and disoriented by the blizzard as he was? His palm curled around a flintlock.

He must have traveled ten feet when the dark blur reappeared a yard in front of him. So swiftly did the creature move that again its identity eluded him, but he did see enough to roughly gauge its size, which was not half as high as his knees and not more than two feet long. A measure of relief fortified him and on he went. Perhaps it was a raccoon or a bobcat, even a rabbit, he speculated. Although why any wild animal would be so close to him was puzzling.

Slowly Nate took in the rope as he ascended. Judging by the weight, the limb under his arm must be a big one, and would be a welcome addition to their dwindling pile. But a single limb, no matter how large, was insufficient for their needs. He would have to make another foray, possibly many more. The thought sparked a shudder.

An interminable interval went by, and Nate swore he had been plodding through the ever-deepening snow for hours when a glimmer of pale light outlined the cleft entrance. Coated liberally with snow, he staggered inside and nearly collapsed with relief.

"Pa!" Zach shouted, coming off the saddle in a rush. "Let me help you."

Ordinarily Nate would have told his son that he could handle the job himself. In his exhausted state he did not argue, but rather helped Zach lower the limb to the floor. Then, shuffling awkwardly, he lumbered to the fire and sank down.

"Are you all right?" Zach inquired anxiously.

"Never felt better," Nate tried to answer, and was shocked by the croaking noises that issued from his throat instead of words.

"Pa?" Zach said, swinging around so he could kneel next to Nate's legs. "What's the matter with you? Why can't you talk?" He placed his hand against his father's cheek. "Tarnation! You're frozen!"

"No," Nate rasped. He had to swallow several times and massage his throat before his vocal cords would work correctly. "I'm fine, son. And I saw your animal."

"You did? What kind is it?"

"I couldn't tell, but it's nothing to worry about." Nate inched nearer the fire, savoring the pleasant tingling in his arms and legs. As an experiment he tapped a finger on his nose but felt no sensation.

"Is there anything I can do?"

"Maybe drag that limb over here and see if you can chop it down to size," Nate requested. The tingling was spreading, growing painful. Grunting, he reclined on his left side, his face to the flames, unwilling to move a muscle until either he thawed completely out or spring came, whichever happened first. He heard Zach begin chopping, a rhythmic thunk-thunk-thunk that lulled him to the verge of sleep. In his nostrils was the spicy scent of burning wood.

With a start, Nate opened his eyes. He knew he had dozed off, and wondered how long he had slept. The fire seemed the same, but Zach's chopping had ceased. Tensing, he rose up on an elbow and glanced over his shoulder to see if the chore had been done. What he saw caused him to scramble awkwardly to his knees and clutch both flintlocks.

"Shhhh, Pa," Zach whispered. "Don't spook it."

"It" was a young wolf, no more than a pup, standing just within the opening with head held low and its thin lips pulled up over its tiny fangs. It glared from Zach to Nate and back again, doing its best to appear as fierce as it could but failing miserably. Size alone did not belie its savagery; the soaked, haggard condition of its fur and its gaunt body did. Its thin legs trembled so hard, the pup shook from nose to tail.

"I was chopping and looked up and there it was," Zach revealed. "It must want in out of the cold real bad."

"Now we have fresh meat," Nate said, easing his left pistol out. Wolf meat wasn't regarded as exceptionally tasty, but as hungry as he was he'd eat it raw.

"No!" Zach yelled, and the pup instantly backed away and twisted, about to flee out into the blizzard. So weak was it that it tripped over its own feet and stumbled against the side of the entrance. "Don't shoot, Pa. Please."

"Why not?" Nate wanted to know.

"I want to keep it."

"You what?"

"Raise it as a pet, just like we did with Samson."

"Samson was a dog," Nate noted, recalling the huge black mongrel that had lived with them for so many years it had been part of the family. All too vividly he remembered Samson's death at the hands of murderous Apaches down near Santa Fe.

"So?"

"So this is a *wolf*," Nate stressed, his finger on the trigger. The pup had stopped and was framed in the opening, as easy a target as he could wish for. One shot, right between the eyes, would . . .

"Drags the Rope raised a wolf once for a couple of years," Zach said. "He said it made a fine pet."

"He did?"

"Yep. Please, let me try to make friends with it."

"Of all the harebrained notions," Nate muttered, wavering between the rumblings of his empty stomach and the silent yet eloquent appeal in his son's eyes. "Just because Drags the Rope took one in doesn't mean this one will take to being domesticated. A wolf is about as wild a creature as walks God's green earth. It has a mind of its own."

"Please, Pa."

"The darn thing will likely try to bite you if you get too close."

"Please."

Nate resisted the impulse to give in. He had their lives to think of. Should the blizzard last for more than three or four days, they'd face the grim specter of starvation. If he had to choose between sacrificing a wretched pup or his son, the outcome was a foregone conclusion.

The wolf made bold to come a few feet nearer, drawn by the heat of the fire. A pitiable whine passed its lips.

"What do you say?" Zach prompted.

Against Nate's better judgment, he slowly lowered the flintlock and shook his head at his own stupidity. "Go ahead," he said wearily, taking solace in two facts. One, they weren't starving yet. And two, if they kept the pup around they could always eat it later.

Chapter Eight

Even as Winona leaped at the shadowy figure, he straightened to his full height, and as her knife streaked at his chest she realized there was only one person in the entire tribe who was so huge. Too late, she attempted to angle her blow away from him, but the blade was so close that the best she could hope to do was bury it in his shoulder. Fortunately, his reflexes were as astounding as his stature, and the keen tip was an inch from his flesh when his enormous hand seized her wrist, checking the swing effortlessly.

"It is I, Winona," Touch the Clouds said. "Not him."

She sagged against him then, overcome by the dreadful mistake so narrowly avoided. Her previous statement that he was like a brother to her was no idle declaration. Since childhood they had been the best of friends, and before Nate came into her life it had been Touch the Clouds who served as her protector as well as his sister's. "I am so sorry," she mumbled.

"I saw you come this way and thought I should make certain he did not bother you," the giant explained, wisely not aggravating her misery by referring to her attack.

"I needed wood."

Touch the Clouds saw the pile. "Let me," he said. Disengaging himself, he walked over and retrieved the limbs. In his arms they looked like twigs.

All the way back to the lodge Winona said nothing, so preoccupied was she. Head bowed, she wrestled with the guilt that assailed her. To think she had almost killed one of her closest friends! She had long prided herself on her ability to deal with any crisis that might arise, and she was devastated by her failure.

At the lodge Touch the Clouds deposited the limbs and stepped back, his dark eyes studying her intently. "Perhaps it would be best if you spent the night with my wife and me."

"I will be fine," Winona said softly, finding the courage to look him in the eyes at last.

"If not us, then with Willow Woman and her husband."

"I do not want to impose on your sister either."

"Neither of us would be bothered. Rather we would be honored that you allow us to look out for you."

"Am I a grown woman or a child?" Winona said petulantly, and in so doing defined the core of her problem. Would she dishonor her family and her husband by falling to pieces, or would she persevere and prove herself worthy of the famous Grizzly Killer? "Please go. I am in no danger."

Like a wraith, Touch the Clouds disappeared in the night, and Winona took her wood inside. Three steps in she abruptly stopped and stared at a neatly folded buffalo robe lying near her fading fire. It hadn't been there when she left, and she knew immediately it wasn't hers.

102

Going forward, she set down the wood and picked up the robe.

Her hands told her this was a new one, the hide in excellent condition. Her mind did not need deductive insight to know who had placed the robe there in her absence. Striding to the opening, she shoved the flap aside, tossed the robe out, and shouted, "When I need a new robe I will ask my *husband* to kill a buffalo for me."

Securing the flap, Winona fed branches to the fire and sank down beside it. She thought of Nate and Zach and wondered where they might be. How she wished they were with her now! But since they weren't, and probably would not show up for some time, she must deal with the situation as she saw fit.

What could she do that she hadn't already done? Winona wondered. She had made her feelings emphatically clear to Jumping Bull, yet he persisted in courting her. So she must continue to ignore him and hope he would not become more aggressive. If he did, she must deal with him accordingly.

The reminder moved her to the wall, where she took a polished pistol from a parfleche and methodically loaded the gun as Nate had instructed her. She had balked when he first proposed teaching her, and was glad he had refused to take no for an answer. In a clash between a man and a woman, where size and strength were decided masculine advantages, a gun equalized things. Jumping Bull would think twice before trying to force his will on her if he knew he risked getting a lead ball in the gut.

Winona tied a rawhide cord around her slim waist and wedged the flintlock under it so it would always be handy. Jumping Bull was devious; whatever he tried, he would do it when she least expected, so she must be ready at all times. Moving to another parfleche, she removed several pemmican cakes and took a seat facing the entrance. As she bit into one she heard a faint snap from outside, possibly made by someone stepping on a twig.

Intuition filled her with foreboding. It might be anyone passing by, but somehow she knew that was not the case. Jumping Bull was out there, keeping an eye on her lodge. Why? Did he intend to sneak in and take her to his lodge against her will? Would he be so reckless? Yes, she realized. He just might.

The pemmican lost its taste, and Winona set the cakes aside to eat later. Rising, she tiptoed to the flap and made doubly sure it was fastened. A strong man might easily break in, but in so doing he would make enough noise to arouse her from slumber. Or such was her hope.

Winona spread out her robe by the fire, put the pistol and the knife within easy reach, and lay on her side, her head cradled on her hands. I must be strong! she told herself. I must not give in to fear or indecision!

She gazed forlornly into the writhing flames, thinking how lonely the lodge was without her loved ones. Memories of the first time she had ever laid eyes on Nate, when he saved her from marauding Blackfeet, stirred her heart. He had charged out of nowhere, putting his life in peril for total strangers, and from the moment she saw him, she was his. She could not explain how it happened; she only knew it had. An indefinable yearning had drawn her to him with irresistible force, and that first night of their acquaintance she had gone walking with him under his robe. Her brazenness, in retrospect, amazed her. Had her grandmother been alive, she would have been reprimanded severely. "Only a woman of loose morals," her grandmother had often intoned, "allows a man to touch her before they are joined together as man and wife." She had sincerely believed those words, yet when the test came, love had prevailed.

Love. What a mystery it was! When her daughter was of age—and she fervently hoped the baby due in eight moons would be a girl—she must remember to be patient with her and to understand that love made people commit acts they would not otherwise contemplate. She must also point out that when two people were meant to be together, no force in the world could keep them apart.

Gradually Winona's eyelids drooped, and the last sound she heard was the howling of the wind as it raged among the lodges with renewed vigor. A storm must be coming, she thought. Then sleep claimed her.

"Isn't he cute, Pa?"

"Wonderful."

"It tickles when he licks my hand."

"I suppose it does."

"Is anything wrong?"

"I'm tired of being cooped up in here. A whole day has passed and it's still snowing."

"But not quite as hard."

"Hard enough to keep us penned in."

"Would you like to play with Blaze for a spell? It might cheer you up."

"Maybe later."

The second morning after the blizzard struck Nate awakened to a peculiar sensation on his face and he lay still, trying to figure out why his cheeks and chin felt wet. The reason was forthcoming seconds later when a moist tongue pressed against his jaw and left a path of cool drool clear up to his forehead. Opening his eyes, he found himself nose to nose with the pup. From nearby came a youthful giggle.

"You're downright hilarious, son," Nate said, sitting up. Without warning, the pup launched itself into his lap and nipped playfully at his shirt. "Now get this critter off me."

"Blaze likes you, Pa," Zach said, taking the skinny wolf in his arms. "After all the jerky you've fed him, you're his friend for life."

"I was trying to put some flesh on his bones in case we needed to . . ." Nate said testily, and suddenly fell silent, aware of a drastic change outside. "The wind has stopped!" he declared. Shoving erect, he dashed to the opening and gazed in breathless awe on a sweeping white vista extending for as far as the eye could see. Snow four to five feet deep covered everything. Not a single blade of grass or weed was visible. Trees laden heavily with clumps of clinging snow were bent under the oppressive weight. Rocks, boulders, logs—they all were buried. It was as if a heavenly artist had painted the landscape white with a single sweep of a celestial brush.

"Isn't it glorious, Pa!" Zach breathed at Nate's elbow.

"Yep." Nate ventured outside, inhaling the fresh, frigid, invigorating air, and craned his neck to scan the sky to the west and the north. A few fluffy white clouds floated sluggishly on the currents. "The storm is finally over," he said thankfully.

"Does this mean we head home right away?"

Nate glanced at the spine, where the elk carcass lay blanketed by thick snow. More than anything he wanted to be on his way to the village, but leaving now would make a mockery of Zach's hunt and leave hundreds of pounds of prime meat to spoil or be devoured by scavengers. "We'll stick to our original plan and butcher the elk first."

"Do Blaze and me get to help cut up the elk?" Zach inquired hopefully.

"Blaze?" Nate said, looking down. The pup stood next to Zach's leg, its tiny black nose twitching as, with tilted

106

head, it tried to catch scents from below. Nate had to admit he'd been surprised at how readily the scrawny beast had taken to the boy. That first night, when Zach had slowly approached with outstretched hand, Nate had expected the wolf to either flee or tear into Zach with all the innate ferocity of its kind. Instead, to his amazement, the pup had sniffed, whined, sniffed some more, and then tentatively licked Zach's fingers.

Now, at Nate's mention of the name that Zach had used so many times the pup already associated the name with itself, the wolf looked up at Nate, its white throat patch bright in the morning sun.

"You'd better keep the pup here," Nate advised. "This snow is so deep it'll drown in the stuff."

"Awww, he'll be lonely all by himself," Zach said, running his fingers over the pup's back.

"You can't carry him and your rifle both," Nate admonished. He saw his son frown, and resting a hand on Zach's arm, he said, not unkindly, "There comes a time when every boy has to accept not being a boy anymore, a time when he has to take on bigger responsibilities than he ever had before." Nate paused. "You're at the age now where I'm going to expect more out of you, and I know you won't let me down. When it's time to work, you have to put your nose to the grindstone and forget about playing and wolf pups and nonsense like that. Do you savvy?"

"I savvy, Pa," Zach responded halfheartedly.

Squinting down at the approximate spot where the elk was hidden, Nate said, "Tell you what I'll do. I'll ride on down there and dig out the carcass so the sun can get at it and thaw the meat a bit. Then the two of us will do the butchering later on."

Zach was not dense. He knew his father had made the suggestion so he would have a little more time to spend with Blaze. "Thanks, Pa. That would be fine."

David Thompson

Saddling Pegasus took but a minute. Nate sat loosely astride the gelding as it moved downward, ready to hurl himself to either side should the horse slip and fall. The brilliance of the snow made him squint. He noticed the surface was as smooth as glass and unmarred as yet by animal prints. His own tracks, those he had made on his half-dozen excursions in search of wood, had long since filled in. So had the big holes he'd made when digging down to locate grass and other forage for the horses.

Nate skirted the ravine this time due to the many large boulders dotting the bottom of it, obstacles he would be unable to see and which might injure Pegasus if the gelding collided with one. Riding a bit further north, he then swung around and rode up the slope of the spine. The going was rough, the snow in places up above the tops of Pegasus's legs.

Both of them were breathing heavily when Nate reined up and slid off. The snow came to his waist. Straining, he plowed to where the elk should be and began scooping with his left forearm. In due course he realized he had picked the wrong spot. Moving a few feet to the right, he tried again.

On the third attempt Nate uncovered a frozen rear leg. Encouraged, he dug until he had exposed the rear half of the kill, then stopped to rest for a minute. Strenuous exertions at extremely high altitudes were exceptionally tiring, and he didn't care to wear himself out so soon, not with the butchering to do.

Nate glanced at the cleft but saw no sign of his son. A survey of the valley showed nothing was moving about. For once, total tranquility reigned in the Rockies, a fleeting interlude he took advantage of. Industriously he dug, and didn't stop until the entire carcass had been uncovered.

Caked with sweat, Nate sat down on the elk and mopped his brow with his sleeve. There was still no sign of Zach. Since he had no desire to ride back up to fetch the boy when Zach was perfectly capable of saddling the mare and following the trail he had broken, Nate cupped a hand to his mouth and bellowed, "Zachary! Do you hear me?"

The words echoed off the high peak far above. Somewhere a bird squawked, as if in reply.

"Zach!" Nate shouted. "Do you hear me?"

Once again the cry bounced off the snow-encrusted summit and seemed to roll out across the valley below.

"He must be playing with that mangy pup," Nate complained under his breath, and rising, he impetuously drew one of his pistols. He had to get Zach's attention, and what better way than with a gunshot? Pointing the barrel into the air, he cocked the hammer, waited a second to see if Zach might yet appear, and when the boy didn't step from the cleft, squeezed the trigger.

For the third time a sharp sound echoed off the top of the mountain.

Nate lowered the flintlock and smiled on seeing Zach dash outside, the wolf on the boy's heels. Beckoning with his free hand, he called up, "Saddle Mary and head on down. We have a heap of work to do."

Before Zach could acknowledge the yell, a tremendous rumbling erupted, coming from the upper reaches of the rocky heights. Nate glanced up and felt a chill pierce his soul. In his annoyed state he had carelessly overlooked a very real, imminent danger, and now he was about to pay the price for his rash folly.

The blizzard had dumped three times as much heavy snow on the higher reaches of the mountain as on the lower slopes. In spots drifts 20 feet high had been sculpted by the whipping winds, and many of these massive drifts were perched precariously over steep inclines. All it would take to send them hurtling down the mountainside with the unstoppable force and deceptive speed of a steam engine were a few sudden, loud noises, as anyone familiar with the high country knew.

Nate knew this. He was fully aware of the risk of an avalanche after a heavy snow, especially above the tree line. But his anger had prompted him to act impulsively, and here, before his anxious eyes, he saw a great crack appear in a vast bank of snow hundreds of feet above. The crack widened rapidly. Resembling distant thunder, the rumbling increased in volume until the ground itself appeared to shake, and a moment later tons of snow tumbled violently downward in a showery spray of white.

"Take cover in the cleft!" Nate screamed at Zach, hoping the din of the onrushing snow wouldn't drown him out. Whirling, he retrieved the Hawken and raced for Pegasus, his legs churning, the elk carcass completely forgotten.

The avalanche was growing quickly in size and ferocity. Much as a snowball grows when rolled down a hill, the avalanche was sweeping up more and more snow and thereby adding to its monumental proportions with every passing foot. Stretching for over a hundred yards end to end, rearing 30 feet in the air, the roiling sheet of choking death cascaded over enormous boulders and dwarf trees and propelled both along with it.

Nate reached Pegasus and vaulted into the saddle. Reining around, he put his heels to the gelding's flanks, making for the cleft. He could see Zach gawking upward. "Get inside!" he screamed. "Inside, where it's safe!"

Zach, apparently, couldn't hear him. Spellbound, the boy watched the awe-inspiring spectacle as crucial seconds ticked by. Then, when the leading edge of the avalanche was less than 50 feet above the cleft, Zach must have seen the peril he was in because he cast a terrified glance at Nate, spun, and ran for the opening.

110

A heartbeat later a swirling wall of snow engulfed Zach and the cleft.

"I tell you that I heard a shot," Bobcat had insisted a minute earlier, and without waiting for his companions, who had been laughing uproariously at a crude joke told by Walking Bear, he had started up through the aspens.

"I heard nothing," Loud Talker said.

"Bobcat's ears are sharper than ours," Walking Bear commented. "Perhaps he did hear something."

Little Dog, in the act of getting his horse ready to leave, gazed at the swiftly moving figure of their friend and sighed. He had not heard anything either, and he doubted very much that Bobcat had. The last thing he wanted was another delay when they were finally about to start for their own country, so he said, "Let us ride out. He will catch up soon."

"No," Rolling Thunder declared. "We must stay together." Lance in hand, he strode upward. Walking Bear and Loud Talker trailed him.

"Wait for me," Little Dog said with no enthusiasm whatsoever. All he wanted to do was go home. Dejected, he followed them, certain Bobcat had heard a limb break under the weight of snow, nothing more. He laughed lightly, bitterly. Except for the killing of the trapper, the whole trip had been a waste of time and energy. But he was the only one who saw it that way. The others, as they'd made clear during their discussions while the blizzard raged, saw their trip into Shoshone country as a great success. Sometimes, he reflected, his friends were utter fools. He swore to himself that this would be the last time he went anywhere with them, although in his heart he knew he didn't mean it.

Suddenly there was an excited shout.

Breaking into a run, or as much of a run as he could manage in the deep snow, Little Dog soon caught up with his companions, all of whom were standing at the edge of the aspens and staring at something much higher up on the mountain.

"It is a white man!" Bobcat exclaimed.

"You are sure?" Rolling Thunder asked doubtfully, taking a step forward.

Then Little Dog spotted the distant figure, but he too could not determine if the rider was white or Indian. Above the rider streaked an avalanche, and to Little Dog's astonishment he realized the rider was heading straight for it. "What is he doing?"

"Committing suicide," Loud Talker said.

"Look!" Bobcat declared. "Now he is fleeing."

In silent fascination they observed the tableau unfold. Being over half a mile to the south of the snowslide, they were well out of harm's way.

"White or not, he will never make it," Rolling Thunder said.

Little Dog had to agree. The avalanche was almost on the rider. Whoever the man was, he was doomed.

"Noooooo!" Nate wailed at the instant his son and the cleft were swallowed by the deluge of snow and debris. Shocked by the horror he had witnessed, he rode in a daze for ten more yards, until his brain awoke to the personal peril he was in from the white maelstrom. The avalanche would soon be on him!

Jerking on the reins, Nate urged Pegasus downward. The gelding floundered, caught itself, and barreled through a drift. Impeded by the clinging snow and the treacherously slippery ground under its driving hoofs, the horse could do no better than a lurching run, try as it might.

Nate looked back, saw the avalanche gaining. Grimly he rode on in the vain hope that if he got low enough the avalanche might bowl him over but would leave him otherwise unscathed. In his ears was a hissing roar, as if a gigantic serpent pursued him. The air vibrated to the beat of invisible hands.

Occasionally Nate had given thought to his own death. Often he had speculated that he would probably be killed by hostiles, or fall to the slashing claws of a great grizzly. Never once had he considered an avalanche as the possible cause of his death, and now, as he girded himself to meet his Maker, he wished it *had* been Indians or a bear that did him in. The end would likely have been swift, in the heat of combat, infinitely preferable to being smothered alive or having every bone in his body broken and lying helplessly paralyzed until starvation or the cold claimed him.

Something slammed into the middle of Nate's back, causing him to fling his arms out, and he was nearly unhorsed. Regaining control of the reins, he hunched low, twisted, and beheld a mammoth rippling wave of snow lapping at the gelding's flying hooves. The sky was blotted out by the curling crest. A heartbeat elapsed. Two. Then, with a muted growl, the avalanche swooped down upon him and enclosed him in its icy grasp. He went sailing head over heels and heard a terrified squeal from Pegasus. On and on and on he flew, flipping like an ungainly acrobat, his limbs flailing wildly, losing his beaver hat and his Hawken. His powder horn, ammo pouch, and possibles bag battered him ceaselessly. He had no idea which way was up, which way was down. He didn't know right from left, or north from south, east from west. Sheathed in the roiling snow, he was totally helpless, his strength as inconsequential before the might of the avalanche as would be that of a gnat trapped in a tornado. Vaguely he was conscious of traveling a great distance. Always he plummeted downward.

Of a sudden, Nate struck a hard object. Stunned, he tried to lift his head to see what it had been, but he slammed into something else. His vision swam. His consciousness faded. Dimly he glimpsed a glimmer of sunlight, or thought he did, and felt himself sliding over a smooth surface, or believed he was. At long, long last he coasted to a stop. Blood was on his tongue. He blinked, attempted to rise, and was sucked into a void more frightening than that of the avalanche. Then all went black.

Chapter Nine

"Your husband and son are both dead!"

Winona stiffened at the belligerent declaration behind her, and slowly lowered the shirt she had been stitching to her lap. Adopting a mocking smile, she faced the lodge entrance and responded casually, "My husband is hard to die, as the white men say. He will be home soon enough, Jumping Bull, and you will have your chance to settle with him. Although"—and she paused deliberately—"were I you, I would pack up my belongings and go live in Canada for the rest of my life."

"Why would I want to live there?" he baited her.

"Living there is better than dying here."

Jumping Bull bristled. "You think your weakling of a husband can slay me? With my own two hands I have strangled a Blackfoot!"

"How many of the mighty humped bears have you killed?" Winona retorted, and hid her delight at the flush that infused the warrior's cheeks. She had no means of preventing him from paying her a dozen visits a day, so she had decided to make each of his visits a poignant lesson in humiliation.

"Mock me while you can, woman," Jumping Bull snapped. "But we both know the high mountains were hit by a blizzard. Our hunters have told us as much. Can your cherished Grizzly Killer kill storms as well?"

Fear blossomed in the depths of Winona's soul. Touch the Clouds had informed her of the reports of heavy snow to the northwest, and she knew Nate had not packed any supplies with him because he had intended to live off the land. She shuddered, thinking of the dire consequences if he and Zach had been caught unawares, and prayed the blizzard had missed them.

"I thought not," Jumping Bull said, noticing, and smiled triumphantly. He crossed his legs, making himself comfortable as was his custom. "We have much to talk over."

"In the next life."

Ignoring her sarcasm, Jumping Bull asked, "Why have Willow Woman and her friends been spreading rumors about me?"

"They have?" Winona said in genuine surprise. It was common knowledge her situation was the talk of the camp, but this was the first she had heard of her friends contributing to the general gossip.

"You know they have. My sister, Rabbit Woman, overheard them saying I had no right to cause so much dissension among our people and that the Yellow Noses should run me off for the good of all."

They should! Winona wanted to say, but didn't. The village was undergoing the worst upheaval in her memory. Men and women were taking sides, with the majority expressing their support for Nate and her, while a small but vocal minority were doing their best to convince everyone else Jumping Bull was in the right. Several heated arguments had occurred, and a pair of warriors, former best friends, had come close to blows. All this among a people who prided themselves on their ability to live together peacefully.

"And they are not the only ones," Jumping Bull was saying. "I do not like what Touch the Clouds, Drags the Rope, and their friends have been doing."

"Which is?"

"They have been trying to decide who should take in my son after your husband returns."

A merry laugh came from Winona's lips. The only reason anyone would adopt Runs Fast would be if Jumping Bull died. Touch the Clouds and the others, by going around broaching the subject when they knew what they said would get back to Jumping Bull, were discreetly putting pressure on Jumping Bull to desist before he wound up dead at Nate's hands.

"I do not find it humorous," he said.

"You would be wise to heed their warning. Or do you want your son to lose his father as he has already lost his mother?" Winona shook her head. "Your hatred has clouded your judgment."

"Do you think less of me because I despise the whites?"

"I do not understand why you hate them so. They have never harmed us. The trappers are our friends."

"Friends!" Jumping Bull exploded. "Are they being friendly when they trap all the beaver from our streams? Are they being friendly when they kill our game? Are they being friendly when they take our women as their wives and then desert the women once they have all the pelts they want?"

"Grizzly Killer will never desert me," Winona said defensively.

"Now whose judgment is clouded? Is your Nate any

different from the rest? Is he more loyal than they? More decent?"

"Yes."

"Waugh!" Jumping Bull said, and spat on the ground. "You are being deceived and you are too foolish to see it." Bending forward, he eyed her craftily. "Answer a question for me."

"Why should I?"

"Prove me wrong. I know your Grizzly Killer has sold many furs at the rendezvous. Tell me that he does not hoard the money he receives."

"He has taught me the value of saving for our future needs. What of it?"

"Heed my words. When he has saved enough, he will take his money and leave you. The whites value their bits of paper and little pieces of metal more than they do life itself."

Winona stared at him in disbelief. "How is it," she inquired, "that one who has lived so many winters, who has married and raised a young son, can be so ignorant of life? I feel sorry for you, Jumping Bear."

The warrior recoiled as if slapped. "I do not want your pity, woman. I want your love. And I *will* have it once I prove to you that I am the better warrior."

"If you kill him, I will hate you forever."

"For a while you will hate me, but in time you will come to see I was right all along. We will grow old together."

Once again their conversation had come full circle, and once again Winona's loathing had been kindled to a fever pitch. She glanced down at her pistol, partially hidden by a fold of her buckskin dress, and felt, stronger than ever, the temptation to pick it up and end her woes by shooting Jumping Bull in the head. But she could not bring herself to do it. She had killed enemies before, yet always when her life or the lives of her loved ones had been at stake. And since Jumping Bull was not threatening her physically right at that moment, she could no more slay him than she could slit the throat of a newborn.

Disappointed in her lack of resolve, Winona looked at the entrance, about to tell Jumping Bull to leave. He had saved her the trouble by having already left. But she knew he would be back.

He always came back.

"I see a hand!" Bobcat yelled, and goaded his perspiring mount across the shimmering slope to where several pale fingers jutted from the cold snow. Leaping down, sinking to his knees, he scrambled to the slack fingers and energetically set to work digging out the person to whom they were attached. In seconds he had the entire hand exposed. "Help me!" he urged. "We do not want him to die before we test his manhood."

"You are wasting your time," Walking Bear said as he reined up. "No one could have survived that avalanche. The man is already dead."

Bobcat continued to dig anyway, spurred by the promise of the thrills he stood to experience if the white man was alive and could be tortured. Of all life's pleasures, Bobcat enjoyed inflicting pain and killing the most. And above all else he enjoyed inflicting pain on and killing white men, the arrogant intruders who presumed to treat the land as if it was their very own, and who had formed alliances with long-standing enemies of the Gros Ventres, such as the Shoshones.

In a flurry of snow Rolling Thunder arrived on the scene and leaped down beside Bobcat. "Let me help you," he said, scooping both of his brawny hands in to the wrists. With a powerful flip of his fingers he excavated a large hole.

"Did either of you see what happened to his horse?" Walking Bear asked. "I want it for my own." Shifting, he studied the swath left by the avalanche, consisting of a jumbled mass of snow and boulders and shattered tree limbs. About 40 yards off, Little Dog and Loud Talker were examining something partially buried in the snow. "I wonder if they found it," he said to himself, and rode toward them.

Rolling Thunder watched him leave, then resumed digging at a frenzied pace. He cared nothing for the stupid horse. It was the man he wanted, a man he hoped was white so he could make up for the blunder he had committed in giving the trapper's hair to Walking Bear. Soon he had dug down to the elbow. Then the hair. Working in concert with Bobcat, he brushed the snow away from the man's head, revealing the face.

"He is white!" Bobcat cried

Touching his fingers to the man's neck, Rolling Thunder found a pulse. "And he is alive."

Shoulder to shoulder, they burrowed downward until the man's chest was clear of the snow. Then each one took an arm, gripped firmly, and heaved. Slowly, laboriously, they pulled the man out, then set him down on his back.

"I hope he is not broken up inside," Bobcat remarked, kneeling to give their captive a thorough going-over. He lifted a limp arm, then a leg, and let both drop.

"Why do you care if the white bastard is hurt?" Rolling Thunder inquired.

"Because I want him to live long enough for me to show him what true pain really is," Bobcat said. "I saw him first, so I will decide what to do with him." He tapped a knot the size of a duck egg on the man's forehead. "I see many bruises, cuts, and scrapes, but his bones do not appear to be broken and he breathes steady."

Rolling Thunder draped a hand on the hilt of his knife. "I want his hair."

"Find your own white dog," Bobcat responded, plucking a pistol caked with snow from under the man's wide belt. "This one is mine."

"I want his hair," Rolling Thunder repeated softly.

Bobcat glanced up, his smile disappearing, his features hardening. "His scalp is mine. I have every right to it. Who saw him first? Who was the first to reach him? His hair will hang in my lodge."

"I want it."

Indignation brought Bobcat to his feet, his right hand closing on his tomahawk. Anyone who led a war party or a hunting party was entitled to express his wishes freely, but the leader was not allowed to dictate to those who accompanied him. "Why should I give such a prize to you? You have done nothing to earn it."

"I know. And I do not dispute that. But if you allow me to claim it, you will have my deepest gratitude."

"I would rather have the scalp."

"Think about this," Rolling Thunder said. He was determined to have his way so he could ride proudly into their village waving the hair from the end of his lance, effectively putting an end to any hope White Buffalo had of challenging him to be the new chief. "Is it not true that one day soon our chief will die and I will become the most important man among our people?"

"Yes. What difference does it make?"

"Would it not be to your benefit to be on friendly terms with me when I have the power to grant you anything you might want? Horses, guns, the woman of your choice—as a chief I can use my influence to help you obtain everything you have ever desired."

Gradually the anger seeped from Bobcat's dark eyes and he relaxed his grasp on the tomahawk. It would be nice, he reflected, to have such influence, especial-

David Thompson

ly when the time came to divide the spoils of future raids. And too, there was a certain woman he liked whose father refused to let him enter their lodge simply because he didn't own as many horses as some of her other suitors. As chief, Rolling Thunder could perhaps persuade the reluctant father that letting Bobcat court the daughter was in the best interests of everyone concerned.

"Well?" Rolling Thunder prompted, sensing victory.

"You can have the scalp," Bobcat declared. He glanced quickly at the others, who were approaching but still 30 feet off, then stepped close to Rolling Thunder and said, "But if you do not honor your words, I will consider you an enemy."

A caustic retort was on Rolling Thunder's tongue, a retort he never uttered. To do so would antagonize Bobcat, who in turn would deny him the scalp. Far better, he reasoned, to overlook the affront for now. After he became chief would be the time to pay Bobcat back. "I always speak with a straight tongue to you. I will honor my words."

"See that you do."

Further conversation was interrupted by the coming of their three companions.

"How is the man?" Little Dog asked, staring at the prone form.

"He survived," Bobcat answered.

"His horse did not. Its neck is broken. We tried moving the body to get at the saddle, but the horse is too heavy."

"I would not want a white man's saddle anyway," Loud Talker said. "They are too soft and uncomfortable." He chuckled. "Do you remember the time White Buffalo killed the trapper and brought back the trapper's saddle? We all were allowed to try it. I thought I was riding on a pile of hides!"

Little Dog nudged the man with the toe of his moccasin. "What do you plan to do with him?"

"I will build a fire and we will test his courage," Bobcat replied.

"Out here in the open?" Little Dog said.

"In the aspens then."

"And delay our return to our village?" Little Dog bobbed his chin northward. "I think it would be wiser to take him with us and do as you want after we have stopped for the night. Remember, we are still in Shoshone country."

"I do not fear them," Bobcat stated.

"Who does?" said Rolling Thunder. "But I agree with Little Dog. We have far to travel and we should go now while the day is young. Tie this white snake on the horse I took from the trapper and we can be off."

"As you wish," Bobcat said docilely, and moved to their mounts.

It was a totally mystified Little Dog who stood aside while the prisoner was bound and gagged and thrown over the back of the animal. Perplexed by Bobcat's highly unusual conduct, he tried to think of a reason. Ordinarily, Bobcat gave in to no man, not even Rolling Thunder, yet here Bobcat had behaved as meekly as a little puppy.

Moments later they were all on their horses and riding, single file, down the slope of the mountain to the less perilous valley floor. Turning northward, they spent the rest of the morning contending with deep drifts and blowing snow. By midday they had covered a bare four miles.

"At this turtle's pace it will take us a full moon to reach our people," Walking Bear groused when they halted to give their mounts a rest.

Rolling Thunder pursed his lips. "The day is growing warm. Tomorrow will probably be warmer. In three

123

sleeps much of the snow will have melted, and before the eighth sleep comes we will be home."

"Home," Little Dog said reverently.

The temperature did climb, but little of the snow had melted by twilight. For hours their horses struggled to make headway. On several occasions where the snow was too deep and the animals floundered, they all dismounted and pulled each horse to firmer footing again. They were a weary band when they made their night camp in a clearing by a stream.

Walking Bear and Loud Talker went into the woods after game while Rolling Thunder and Bobcat attended to the animals. Little Dog collected wood and soon had a fire crackling. As he arranged the branches to his satisfaction, he heard a low groan and turned to see the white man open his eyes and blink.

"You would have spared yourself much misery if you had died," Little Dog commented, and could tell by the other's expression that the man did not comprehend his tongue. The trapper studied him most carefully, and Little Dog was impressed to note a complete absence of fear. Leaning over, he yanked the gag out.

The man spoke in a strange, musical language.

"I cannot talk like a bird," Little Dog said. "And I do not know Shoshone." An idea goaded him into gesturing in sign language. "My name is Little Dog. I am Gros Ventre. Do you understand?"

Again the man spoke and motioned with his bound wrists.

"Yes, I think you do," Little Dog said. Moving to the trapper's side, he lifted the man's arms so he could get at the knots under the wrists.

"Stop!"

Pausing, Little Dog pivoted as Bobcat hastened up. "He knows sign language," said Little Dog. "We can question him if his hands are untied."

"I did not bring him with us so we could *talk* to him," Bobcat said. "There is nothing he might say that would interest me." Leering, he suddenly kicked the trapper in the stomach, doubling the man over in anguish. "All I want is to hear him scream when I gouge out his eyes and cut off his ears."

Although disappointed, Little Dog left and devoted himself to building the fire higher. He was curious to learn about the white way of life and to hear what had brought this trapper so far from the white world into the land of the Shoshones. Unlike his friends, he had long suspected that the whites were much like his own people in many respects and that if the two sides could sit down and discuss their differences, a peace might be worked out. The Gros Ventres, though, did not make peace with their enemies. They exterminated them.

Bobcat walked off again, and out of the corner of his eye Little Dog saw the trapper surreptitiously appraise each of them. He liked that. Some captives, knowing the fate awaiting them, would have yelled or pleaded, but not this one. This man used his brain; he was taking their measure and perhaps trying to think of a means of escaping. Sadly for someone so brave, there was none.

Presently Loud Talker and Walking Bear showed up bearing a rabbit. Rolling Thunder and Bobcat came and sat by the fire. Little Dog listened as they joked and recounted battles they had been in and told about wild beasts they had slain. He bided his time until Walking Bear glanced at the captive and asked whether anyone had tried to communicate with him.

"I did," Little Dog answered. "He knows sign language. But Bobcat does not want his hands freed."

"Why not?" Walking Bear asked. "It will be amusing to let him spew his lies, and we have nothing else to do."

125

"We will soon be very busy," Bobcat said, glaring at the trapper. "He dies when we are done eating, and all of you can have a hand in it."

"Why rush?" Walking Bear inquired. "Our journey back is a long one." He scratched his chin, pondering. "If I had caught a white man, I would rather take him back to the village for all the people to see. No one has ever done that before. Think of the songs the women would sing of my prowess!"

"I would do the same," Loud Talker mentioned.

The ensuing silence was broken by Rolling Thunder. "Some might say it is bad medicine to bring a white man into our village. Better that he die before we reach our land." He stared across the fire at the object of their disagreement. "But like Walking Bear I am interested in learning what this dog will tell us."

"Then so be it," Bobcat abruptly declared. He crouched by the captive and worked long and hard at the tight knots before they parted. Eyeing the trapper with contempt, he backed up and remarked, "Now make fools of yourselves."

All of them were surprised when Rolling Thunder shot upright, stalked around to the white man, and leaned close to the man's face. "How are you known?" he signed with sharp gestures.

The trapper never batted an eye. "I am called Grizzly Killer," he answered in flawless sign language.

Rolling Thunder took a quick step back, as if he had been punched, then raised his face to the heavens and smiled at the sparkling stars. His prayers had been answered! He clenched his fists and shook them in exultation.

Little Dog and the rest exchanged glances. Of them all, Little Dog was the only one who correctly guessed why Rolling Thunder was acting so oddly. He shifted his gaze to the white man, admiring the man's composure. The stories that whites were all craven cowards were clearly not true.

Grizzly Killer scanned them and fastened on Little Dog. "What happened to my horse?" he inquired.

"It was killed," Little Dog said, and added, "I could see that it was a fine animal."

"The Nez Percé gave it to me," Grizzly Killer signed, his mouth curling downward. "I will miss it."

Bobcat laughed. His fingers and arms flew. "You will not be alive along enough to miss it, bastard! I, Bobcat, am going to cut out your heart and piss on it."

"How many will hold me down when you do?" Grizzly Killer retorted.

In a flash Bobcat was up and at the captive, his knife streaking from its sheath and spearing at the white man's throat. Twisting, Grizzly Killer evaded the thrust, caught Bobcat's wrist, and jerked, sending Bobcat sailing over him to sprawl in an undignified heap in the snow. Grizzly Killer shoved to his knees, his movements slowed by his bound ankles, and turned awkwardly to face Bobcat. As he did, Rolling Thunder stepped in close and swung the butt end of his lance, striking Grizzly Killer on the temple. Soundlessly, the white man crumpled, and the next instant Bobcat was poised above him with the gleaming knife held aloft for a fatal stab.

Chapter Ten

As young Zachary King turned and saw the terrifying vision of the avalanche sweeping down the steep mountain slope toward him, a wave of fear bathed his body from head to toe and he stood rooted in fright to the spot outside of the cleft. He knew he should move, should dash through the opening before the snow struck him, but he could not seem to make his limbs obey his mind. Dimly he heard his father shouting. Closer and closer came the gigantic, turbulent mass, until with a sinking feeling in his gut he knew the avalanche would engulf him in another few seconds. That was when the pup whined.

"Blaze!" Zach cried, roused from his shock. Horrified at the thought of the wolf being killed, he was galvanized into action. He cast a glance at his father far below, then moved to grab the pup by the scruff of its neck, but it darted into the opening on its own. He promptly followed.

No sooner did Zach gain the shelter of the cleft than he was roughly hurled from his feet by an invisible hand that slammed into him from behind. Flying forward, he hit the floor hard and slid to a stop. A peculiar hissing arose. Zach put his hands flat, pushed up, and turned.

Once again terror seized him. Snow was streaming in the entrance and spilling out over the dirt floor, fanning to the right and the left. Frantically Zach backed up. He was afraid the snow would fill the whole interior and smother him.

The wolf stayed at his side. Legs spread, hair bristling, it snarled at the seething spray as if trying to frighten the snow into stopping.

Zach gulped and wished his father was there. His father! "Pa!" he cried, feeling new fear, but not for himself this time. His father had been out in the open, exposed and helpless to avoid the avalanche. What would happen when . . . ?

Shaking his head, Zach refused to give the matter any consideration. "Pa will be all right," he said softly. "He *has* to be." His own problem was more important at the moment. Already several inches of snow covered the ground near the opening.

Unexpectedly, the spray ended, the hissing ceased. A muted, rapidly fading roar showed the avalanche had passed and was rolling on down the mountain.

"Pa!" Zach yelled, running to the entrance. He attacked the snow with his hands, digging furiously, but soon realized the snow was too tightly packed to be easily dug aside. Stepping back, he glanced up at the top of the opening. There appeared to be less snow higher up, so girding his legs he started up the short incline, digging in his moccasins to gain extra purchase.

At the bottom of the pile the wolf uttered a tentative whimper.

"Don't fret, boy," Zach said. "I ain't about to leave

you. But if I don't get us dug out, we'll never see the light of day again."

He reached the apex of the crack and began scooping out handfuls, the snow cold on his palms and fingers. Outside all was now as quiet as a tomb, and the silence made him shiver. "Please let him be all right, Lord," he said. "Please, please, please."

Zach had a lump in his throat as he continued digging. Part of his apprehension was for his father; part was for his own welfare. If anything had happened to his pa—and simply framing the words in his mind was so painful he cringed—what would then happen to him? How would he survive on his own? He glanced over his shoulder at the mare, standing calmly in the back corner, munching on grass his father had brought the day before, as unconcerned as if she was in a stable somewhere. "Stupid horse," he muttered.

For how long Zach dug, he could not say. He made a deep hole in the snow, but still saw no hint of daylight. His fingers became numb, compelling him to halt for a while. Dejected, he carefully climbed down and went to the fire. Blaze followed him.

"We're in for it now, little fellow," Zach said, fighting back tears. He held his hands close to the low flames, barely noticing the warmth. "If I don't find my pa, I don't think I can ever make my way home again."

Blaze lay down with his pointed chin resting on his small paws, and regarded the boy with an expression that could only be described as one of tender affection.

"But I'll bet you Pa made it to safety," Zach went on, bobbing his head. "Yep! I'll bet he did. There isn't nothing my pa can't do."

An ember popped in the fire.

"I never expected anything like this to happen," Zach said, so worked up he was unable to keep from speaking. "I mean, I know bad things can happen in the mountains.

Tenderfoot

Pa is always telling me to stay alert, to always be on the lookout for hostiles and grizzlies and such. He says the wilderness is no place for greenhorns. A man has to know the ways of the animals and the Indians and, most of all, the ways of Nature, if he's to live to a ripe old age like Uncle Shakespeare has done." He paused, suddenly all choked up. "But I'm not no man, Blaze"

Zach lowered his head and stifled a sob of despair. How could he ever hope to measure up to his pa's expectations? Twice now he had been so scared he had nearly leaked in his britches, first when the panther had attacked, and then minutes ago when the avalanche had swarmed toward him. He must be yellow. Why else had he been so darned afraid?

Morosely, Zach stared into the lowering flames and lamented his sorry lot in life. To be born a coward to a man like Grizzly Killer! He'd always taken immense pride in his father's accomplishments, and he'd looked forward to the day when he would prove his worth as a man, when he too would prove he was a brave Shoshone warrior. But cowards were not permitted to go on raids. Cowards were assigned to the ranks of the women and forced to do the same work the women did. They were the laughingstocks of the tribe, shunned by any man who had ever counted coup.

"Oh, Lord," Zach said, almost sorry the avalanche had *not* killed him.

Blaze touched his damp nose to the boy's hand.

"Not now," Zach said. He took a deep breath and felt a slight dizziness. Pressing a hand to his brow, he waited for the spell to pass, then laughed. "Look at me! I'm so scared I'm about to pass out."

Mary whinnied softly.

Zach idly gazed at her and saw her head drooping. "Now what's the matter with you, stupid?" he asked. He flexed his fingers, ascertained they were warm enough for him to go back to digging, and stood. But he managed only a single stride before he halted and swayed as a second bout of dizziness made everything spin. "Oh!" he exclaimed, reaching out for support that wasn't there. He tottered, nearly fell. Seconds elapsed and the dizziness went away, leaving him shaken and experiencing a queasy sensation in his stomach.

"What the dickens is the matter with me?" Zach asked. He glanced at Mary, whose sides were heaving, then at the fire, at the flames that had been reduced to the size of his little finger. "What's happening?" he wondered aloud.

Suddenly Zach remembered! His pa had once given him a lesson on the basics of getting a fire going. "Flames are just like you and me," his father had said. "They need air or they'll smother and die."

Comprehension sent a chill down Zach's spine. There was little air left in the cleft, and unless he dug them out quickly they would all perish. Swiftly he sprang to the mound and clawed his way upward. More dizziness gnawed at his mind, but he steeled his will against it. If he collapsed, he was dead.

Fingers and hands a blur, Zach dug and dug and dug, heedless of where he threw the snow. The wolf tried to stand close to the incline, but was driven back by the rain of clumps. Mary, leaning against the wall, watched the boy.

At length Zach had a small tunnel excavated, yet still there was no glimmer of bright light beyond the snow in front of him. Frustrated, he sank his right hand in to the wrist and tried to pull more snow back. But there was even less air in the tunnel, and the next moment he found himself on his face, gasping loudly, his mind totally awhirl.

"No!" Zach cried. He must not give in when so much was at stake! There was more than his own life to think of; there was Blaze, Mary, and most of all his pa. "Get up, you weakling!" he chided himself, and used a word his parents frowned on. "Damn you, you good-for-nothing!"

Somewhere Zach found a slender shred of strength. Rising on his hands and knees, he thrust both hands into the snow, bunched his shoulders, and wrenched. He expected the snow in front to give way. Instead, without warning, the whole roof caved down on top of him, knocking him flat.

In a panic, Zach screamed and clawed at the clammy coffin embracing him. He kicked wildly. His arms pumped. His heart beat like a drum in his ears. In a frenzied fit he got to his knees and tried to back up, to get out of the tunnel before more snow crashed down on him. A brilliant shaft of light struck him in the eyes and he instinctively raised a hand to block the glare as he scrambled rearward.

The significance of the light brought Zach up short. Slowly, he lowered his arm and sat up, amazed to see blue sky above, a white slope below, and bent aspens laden heavy with snow further down. "I did it!" he blurted out. Ecstatic, he took deep breaths and stumbled to his feet. "I did it!"

Then Zach remembered his father. He anxiously surveyed the slope but saw nothing moving. *"Pa!"* he shouted. "Where are you?"

There was no answering cry.

Fearing the worst, Zach moved away from the hole. His left leg bumped something and he bent his head to discover Blaze at his feet. "So you followed me out, did you?" he said, glancing back. The cave-in had created a tunnel over three feet high and two feet wide. Plenty of air would reach Mary.

Zach hiked lower. He spotted a large, dark object protruding from the snow lower down and off to the

133

north. "Please, no," he prayed, and broke into a run, the snow able to bear his weight where it would have crumpled under the heavy tread of an adult.

The wolf trotted alongside him.

They were yet 15 yards away when Zach recognized the body as being that of a horse, and from the pied markings on the hindquarters he knew which horse. "Pegasus!" he called forlornly, and ran faster, so fast he collapsed out of breath next to the dead steed and clasped his arms to his stomach. "Pa liked you," he said softly.

A scan of the slope showed only a sea of snow. After a while Zach rose and swept his gaze over the lower portions of the mountain, but there was only more of the same. Moving in a circle, he looked and looked and grew more despondent with each passing minute. His pa, he figured, must have been buried alive. Then he glanced at the snow at his feet.

It took a few seconds for the tracks to register as such; they were so deep the impressions left by the hoofs at the bottom of the holes were difficult to discern. Startled, Zach turned and saw many more fresh horse prints and marks where the animals had slid now and then. He saw where a group of riders had emerged from the aspens, some going directly to Pegasus, the others to a point about 40 yards away.

"What's over yonder?" Zach mused aloud, and ran to see. There he found a hole, a lot more tracks, and a trail leading to the north. Hope flared as he reconstructed what had happened. "There's seven or eight of them, Blaze. Indians too,'cause their horses aren't shod. They must have dug my pa out and taken him with them, and they wouldn't have gone to all that trouble unless he was still alive." Thrilled to his core, he jumped into the air and laughed merrily. "My pa is alive!"

A moment later Zach had sobered. "But what do I

do now?" he wondered. "Since they're heading north, they can't be Shoshones. There ain't no friendly tribes up that way." He paced back and forth, a hand on his chin. "The first thing I have to do is get me a branch and dig Mary out. Then we're going after Pa, Blaze, and if those Indians have hurt him, I aim to make them pay."

He tramped toward the nearest aspens, the wolf padding as always at his side. Halfway there, struck by a devastating thought, he stopped and stared timidly in the direction the abductors of his father had taken. Here he was, a mere sprout of a boy, about to pit himself against a half-dozen skilled enemy warriors. He must be touched in the head to believe he had a realistic chance of saving his pa.

"I'm only a boy," Zach whispered into the wind. "I can't do the impossible." Dejected, he stared up at the cleft, and remembered he had left his rifle inside by the fire. "See?" he addressed the wolf. "I don't even have brains enough to keep my rifle with me at all times like Pa said."

Mechanically Zach moved on, the weight of the world bearing down on his shoulders. There were certain limits to what he could do, he realized. Rescuing his pa was a job for a grown man. He considered trying to find the Shoshone village and alerting Touch the Clouds and the others so they could chase the hostile band, but he knew that by the time he reached the village—if he did—the band would be long gone, the trail long cold.

"No," Zach said, "if Pa's to be saved, then someone has to go after him now. And I'm the only one who can do it. Me. Zach King."

Then Zach thought of his other name, the Indian name bestowed on him by his folks shortly after his birth. "Me. Stalking Coyote," he said dolefully to the pup. Although he had never admitted as much to his parents, he'd never been especially fond of that name since he'd always rated coyotes as rather low in the animal kingdom. Grizzlies and panthers were far more formidable, wolves far more regal, foxes far more intelligent. The only traits coyotes possessed worth admiring were a certain dogged persistence in the pursuit of prey and crafty dispositions. The tricksters, some called them, for the way they often outsmarted badgers and other predators; if a coyote came on a badger in the act of trying to dig a rodent out of its burrow, the coyote would then find the rodent's escape hole and wait patiently there for the noisy digging of the badger to drive the rodent right out into its mouth.

Zach grinned at the recollection. "Now if only I was that tricky," he declared, and lines furrowed his brow as he recalled how once, after he'd won a game he and some of the Shoshone children had been playing, one of the boys had come up to him and complimented him by saying he was the trickiest boy in the whole tribe. "Maybe I am," he now commented.

But trickiness wasn't everything. Only someone with a vast store of wilderness skills could hope to save his pa. The notion made him stop. Hadn't he learned all about survival from warriors who were masters at doing so? He'd made it a point to learn all he could, prompted by advice his Uncle Shakespeare had given him years ago during a talk about Zach's wish to become a great warrior: "You will be one day, Zachary. You've got a sharp mind, as sharp as your pa's, and you can see what he's made of himself. The secret to getting on in life is to always listen and learn from your betters, then go out and apply what they've taught you. And the more you practice at it, the better you'll get, until one day you'll wake up a growed man, a respected warrior of the tribe, and a credit to your family."

So maybe, Zach reflected, he already had the knowledge he needed; he just had to go out and apply it.

With renewed confidence he hurried lower. Among the aspens—where in spots the snow had drifted deep, and in other spots only inches of snow covered the ground— he found a suitable branch. This he toted to the cleft, and once there he had to sit and rest.

"I'm going to make my pa proud," Zach announced to Blaze. "I'm going after him, and I'll fetch him back if it's the last thing I ever do."

Once Zach was refreshed from his climb, he turned to the tunnel and set to work enlarging it, using the branch as a lever to pry large chunks of snow loose. Gravity would then take over, tumbling the snow down the slope. In this fashion he cleared an opening large enough for a man to walk through in not quite half an hour.

Fatigued from his labors, Zach went inside, fed the last of the grass to Mary, and rekindled the fire. Warmth filled the cleft and brought renewed life to his chilled body. Relishing the comfort, he sat with his arms draped around his bent knees and his chin on his wrists. His eyelids became leaden. Twice he started and sat up, only to slump wearily down again.

The next thing Zach knew, he opened his eyes and realized to his horror that he'd fallen asleep. Upset that he could be so careless when his father's life was at stake, when every precious moment counted, he leaped to his feet and applied himself to the snow blocking the opening.

When, eventually, Zach stopped, his shoulders were throbbing and his arms ached, but he had excavated a gaping cavity of which he could be rightfully proud. There was no time to savor his feat, however. Tossing the branch down, he saddled the mare and led her out into the bright sunlight.

Blaze tagged along, sitting when Zach stopped. The boy thoughtfully regarded the wolf, then remarked, "If I leave you here, you might not live out the week. You're too little to get by on your own. But you're also too little to keep up with Mary, so I reckon there's only one thing I can do."

Turning, Zach opened the pair of parfleches hanging on the mare behind the saddle. He removed extra leggins and a spare buckskin shirt from the one on the near side and crammed them into the one on the far side. A few other items were also transferred into the second pouch; then it was closed.

"How are you going to take to this?" Zach wondered as he gently lifted the wolf and nestled it in the first parfleche. He had left just enough room for the pup's head to stick out, and it showed no display of fear as he climbed up and took the reins in his left hand. The Kentucky rifle was in his right.

"Well, here we go," Zach said, clucking the mare into motion. He repeatedly checked the wolf to see if it would thrash around or try to jump out. Thankfully, Blaze did neither, so Zach concentrated on his riding, avoiding steeper sections of the slope where Mary might fall. Presently he was moving northward as rapidly as the mare dared safely go.

Zach was immensely pleased with what he had done so far. He figured he was five to six hours behind the band of hostiles, which made overtaking them before nightfall unlikely. The next day should be different. Since they had no idea they were being chased and would consequently take their time, he should come on them before the second night fell.

The golden sun arced higher in the tranquil blue vault of sky. Zach was hungry, but refused to stop to eat. He was thirsty, but when he came on a thin ribbon of water meandering from west to east, he let the mare and the wolf drink heartily, and only took a few sips of the freezing cold water himself. "Never drink too much when you're out in the wild," his father had counseled.

"Doing so can give you a bellyache or make you outright sick, and a sick man alone is easy pickings for unfriendly Indians and beasts alike."

Zach remembered other lessons as well. He avoided looking directly at the sun to measure the passage of time, which could harm his eyes, and instead gauged how long he had been in the saddle by the lengths of the shadows. He also squinted constantly in order to reduce the glare and spare him from being struck by snow blindness. When he began to sweat, he didn't open his shirt or remove his hat, which would have brought on an attack of the chills after the cold mountain air turned his sweat to ice. Quite a few greenhorn trappers had been found frozen solid, victims of their ignorance of the deadly combination of cold wind and perspiration. A man grew so cold so fast, there was no time to even build a fire.

Zach also scanned for hawks and eagles to the north. Often, when birds of prey spotted something below them that aroused their curiosity, they would glide in tight circles above it until their interest was satisfied. If he should see one doing that now, it might be studying the Indians who had taken his father. None of those he saw, though, circled.

By late afternoon Zach was on the lookout for a spot to stop. He didn't much like the prospect of having to dig down through the snow to find grass for the mare, yet he recognized that if she died, he would too. Whatever was required to keep her alive, he must do.

Fickle fate smiled on the boy. He crested a low hill, wound down into a narrow valley which had been sheltered from the brunt of the blizzard, and turned from the trail into a quiet corner where he found a spring and a tract of ground that had received just a light dusting. With the sun perched above the jagged peaks to the west, he opted to halt.

Everything was done exactly as his pa had taught him. First he attended to Mary, removing his saddle and watering her. He was tempted to let her roam free so she could eat where she chose, but so many times had he heard his father or one of the other mountain men remark that "it's better to count ribs than tracks," that he tied her securely so she would be right there when he wanted her in the morning.

Zach built his fire Indian-style, and warmed himself a short while before taking his rifle and going after game. The hostiles were so far ahead he need not fear the shot being heard. Blaze at his heels, he trudged toward a snow-shrouded meadow where he hoped to find wildlife. So hungry was he that he'd settle for a bird, if such should be all he found.

Suddenly Zach heard a crackling in the brush off to the right and he swung around, leveling the Kentucky, hoping it was a deer or a rabbit. His mouth watered in anticipation that changed to utter terror when, an instant later, into the open lumbered a monster grizzly.

Chapter Eleven

Zachary King went pale and took a step backward, on the verge of fleeing. His pa had told him about the grizzly that visited their camp in the dead of night, and he suspected this was the same bear since grizzlies were known to range over a wide area in their ceaseless quest for food. The deep snow meant nothing to the great brute covered with thick hair and fat put on for the lean winter months ahead.

As Zach started to turn, he paused, recalling yet another tidbit of information gleaned from his father. "Never run from a bear, son. That's what its prey usually does, so when it sees something running away the bear naturally goes after it. Stand your ground, or back away slowly. And don't take your eyes off it. There are some folks who claim bears are afraid of the face of man, that they won't attack you if you stare them down. I don't put much stock in such tales, but it's plain good sense not to turn your back to something that wants to eat you."

So Zach now faced the mighty bruin, his thumb on the rifle hammer. He preferred to go down fighting rather than being taken from behind like an errant coward.

About 20 yards off, the grizzly had halted and was regarding the boy intently. Raising its huge head, the bear sniffed the breeze, trying to detect his scent.

Zach realized the wind was blowing from him to the grizzly, which should be to his advantage. Often bears fled at the smell of man, and since this one had left him unmolested the night of its visit, it might do so again. Yet to his dismay, the monster grunted and moved toward him, its enormous muscles rippling under its fur.

Quickly Zach sighted. He would have time for one shot, then flee to the closest tree and climb like a squirrel to the safety of the highest branches. Grizzlies were too heavy to climb, but they were exceptionally tall, this one looking to be about eight feet when fully erect, with a reach of another three feet, not counting the long claws. Meaning somehow he had to climb over 11 feet in the two or three seconds it would take the bear to reach the tree.

Zach touched his forefinger to the trigger and tensed his finger to squeeze. Unexpectedly, an eerie howl erupted at his very feet, the wavering, ear-piercing wail of a wolf, so startlingly loud that Zach jumped. He glanced down, hissed, "Shush, Blaze!" then glanced at the grizzly.

On hearing the howl the bear had abruptly stopped. Now it backed off to one side, venting an angry growl.

Blaze howled louder, as if crying for his mother.

With a disgusted toss of its head, the grizzly whirled and ran into the brush, vanishing in seconds.

Just like that the encounter was over.

A reaction set in, causing Zach to tremble as he lowered the hammer. Blaze still howled, and he didn't object.

The foolish wolf had inadvertently saved both of their hides. After an anxious minute spent scouring their vicinity to be certain the grizzly was gone, he knelt, grinned, and embraced Blaze with his right arm, holding the now silent animal so tight he swore he could feel the frantic beating of its little heart.

"You did good, boy," Zach said, and was licked on the cheek in return. "I'm right glad you're with me. I don't know how I'd hold up if you weren't."

Rising, Zach pointed due west. "That's the way the bear went." He turned to the east. "So we'll go this way. No need to invite trouble, as Pa always says."

The near-tragic incident made Zach feel oddly light-hearted. He'd met the scourge of the Rockies and lived to tell of it! His confidence was further fortified, and there was a slight swagger in his stride as he hunted, a swagger that became more pronounced after he stumbled on and shot a rabbit.

Countless times had Zach eaten rabbit, yet this one tasted better than any he'd ever known. He lingered over every morsel, chewing with gusto while reviewing the deeds of the day. Ultimately, he decided his fears had been groundless, that if he applied himself, and most of all if he used his head, he would be able to meet the wilderness on its own terms and come out the winner. Or, as he phrased it to Blaze, "Living off the land ain't so tough if you have half a brain."

His elation carried him through an untroubled sleep, and on through the next morning until he found where the Indians had made their first camp. There, as he walked about familiarizing himself with the tracks as his father had taught him to do, he saw something which made his heart skip a beat and his breath rasp in his throat.

It was a small frozen puddle of blood.

*   *   *

Nate King wanted to kill.

He sat astride the horse to which he had been tied, blood trickling from the left corner of his mouth and seeping from his nose, his chin split open, nasty bruises discoloring most of his face, and glared at the Gros Ventre who was leading his mount. Bobcat, they called him, and Nate wanted nothing so much as the opportunity to clamp his brawny hands on Bobcat's throat and squeeze until the son of a bitch turned purple.

But weakness pervaded his body, reminding Nate that he couldn't throttle a rabbit, let along a healthy warrior. He shifted position to relieve an annoying cramp in his right thigh, and winced as sharp pains lanced through his chest. Several of his ribs must be broken, or at the very least fractured. His stomach ached constantly from having been without food since his capture. And his lips were parched and puffy, only partly because his captors wouldn't let him have a drink; the puffiness had been caused by all the blows to the face he had received.

Four of the five Gros Ventres had used every stop to beat mercilessly on him, taking turns punching and kicking and slapping him until they tired of the sport. Of the four, Bobcat was the worst. The warrior became like a madman, striking Nate repeatedly until Nate collapsed from the ordeal. Then Bobcat would throw snow on Nate's face to revive him and begin the torment all over again. It was Bobcat who, the night before, had kicked and kicked until Nate thought his ribs were about to cave in.

Yet Nate was powerless to prevent the Gros Ventres from having their way. His hands were always kept tied behind his back, and whenever they stopped for any length of time his ankles were also securely bound.

While on the move, Bobcat always held fast to the rope used to guide Nate's horse.

Nate gingerly touched the tip of his tongue to his lower lip, and grimaced at the pang that shot along his jaw. He would be lucky if he was ever able to talk again! The thought made him snort lightly at his unwarranted optimism. Being able to talk was the least of his worries. Of more immediate concern was living out the day.

The Gros Ventres had made no secret of the fact they were going to kill him, and they had also let him know they intended to take their time doing so. Bobcat, in particular, liked to brag of the tortures he would inflict on Nate over the next several days. Apparently, they wanted him dead for some reason before they reached their village, but they were going to keep him alive until a day or two before they got there so they could have more fun with him.

Nate wished he had his weapons. He longed for a fighting chance. That was all he asked. But he might as well wish for a fortune in gold because there was no denying the inevitable. He was going to die, and he knew it.

The certainty had been difficult to accept the first day, when Nate had instinctively balked at the notion of being killed in the prime of his manhood. He had seen enough of the wild to know that all forms of life tenaciously cling to their existence, as evidenced by the fierce struggle a rabbit would put up against a panther, or the efforts of a lowly frog to escape the clutches of a snake that was swallowing it alive. To the very last that frog would thrash and kick in a futile attempt to avoid its doom. And humankind, in this respect, was no different from the animals.

Nate wanted to live. Lord, how he wanted to live! He wanted to see his wife again and help her live through the sorrow of Zach's death. He wanted to be there when their second child was born, and his keenest regret was for poor Winona, who had finally been blessed with new life within her after years of longing for an addition to their family. Now she would have to raise the child alone, or perhaps she would marry one of the Shoshone warriors.

The likelihood didn't disturb Nate as much as he would have expected. Men and women were not meant to go through life alone, and he'd rather she found some-one else than spend the remainder of her days mourning him and withering into old age.

Oh, Winona! Nate cried in his mind, and bowed his head in sorrow. He wearily closed his eyes, started to sway, and jerked his eyes open again. If he dozed off he might fall, as had happened once before, and the Gros Ventres would let him hang until they made their next stop, as they had done the last time. For hours he had bounced and flounced upside down over the rough ter-rain, his body occasionally battered by the hoofs of the horse.

Damn their hides all to hell! Nate thought, and glanced back at the others. Directly behind him was the leader of the band, Rolling Thunder, an arrogant brave who always smirked whenever he caught Nate's eye, like now. Nate gazed past Rolling Thunder at the next man, the quiet one known as Little Dog, the only one of the bunch who did not derive enjoyment from inflicting pain on him. Little Dog had not beaten him once. Why not? he wondered. He'd noticed Rolling Thunder had been treating Little Dog with cool reserve, and guessed the two were at odds over something, but he had no idea what it might be.

Nate waited for Little Dog to look his way so he could smile at him, but the warrior was preoccupied and had his attention idly fixed on the ground. A desperate man will clutch at any straw, and Nate's straw was a feeble hope that Little Dog would take pity on him and perhaps set him free late at night so he could sneak off. He knew the hope was ridiculous, yet he entertained it nonetheless.

Facing front, Nate surveyed the landscape ahead. They were coming down out of the mountains onto a wide plain that stretched to the northern horizon, a new region which Nate had never visited before. There was no snow here. Grazing far out were scattered clusters of buffalo and antelope.

As they rode from the forest into the high grass, Nate spotted a coyote to the west. Intense misery racked him and he almost blacked out. In his mind's eye he saw again his young son standing before the cleft as the monstrous avalanche bore down on the boy. The moment was branded indelibly in his memory, and he relived the horror of it countless times each hour.

Such an innocent idea—to take Zach off on his first elk hunt—had resulted in such heartbreaking tragedy! Had Nate been alone he would have buried his head in his arms and sobbed until his tears ran dry. Zach had been his pride and joy, his precious firstborn, the living legacy he had expected to leave on the Earth after he went on to meet his Maker, the precocious promise that the King name would persist through future generations and live to see whatever glorious destiny awaited the human race. Or so Nate had imagined in his flights of fancy.

Now dark and somber depression cloaked Nate's soul and made him exceedingly bitter. He'd been a reckless fool to take Zach off alone, and the boy had paid the ultimate price for his foolishness. Staring skyward, he thought, "Can you ever forgive me, son?" and moisture made his eyes glisten. Overcome by remorse, he sank his chin to his chest, and paid no attention as the Gros Ventres rode on across the plain.

David Thompson

* * *

The incident Winona had feared would occur took place when her guard was down.

For two sleeps Jumping Bull had not bothered her, had not shown up once at her lodge to taunt her, had not offered her unwanted presents. For two days she had enjoyed peace and quiet, and she had about convinced herself that Jumping Bull had seen the error of his ways and decided to stop courting her in order to avoid bloodshed. Or so she hoped.

Then came the third day. Most of the men were gone from the village, off hunting buffalo. Winona had seen them depart early that morning, and among them had been Jumping Bull, Touch the Clouds, and Drags the Rope. Touch the Clouds had smiled and nodded at her, but Jumping Bull, oddly enough, had completely ignored her.

About midday Winona decided to check the snares she maintained in the forest to the northeast of the village. With Nate gone, she had to rely on her own resources in order to obtain fresh meat, and since she refused to impose on her relatives or friends, she resorted to the snares. Her mother had taught her how to make them and how to find rabbit runs and other small game trails when she was still a youngster, and over the years she had perfected her technique to where she now supplied almost as much meat as Nate did.

Taking her knife, an empty parfleche, and a lance that had belonged to her father, Winona strolled through the quiet encampment and into the cool shade of the forest. She should have checked the snares every day, but she had been loath to venture far from the village for fear of what Jumping Bull might do.

Winona didn't fear for herself; she was afraid for Nate and the consequences to her family if she was molested. As things now stood, since Jumping Bull had not laid a hand on her, the dilemma might be resolved without violence. But if Jumping Bull did touch her, Nate's wrath would be uncontrollable; he'd slay Jumping Bull, and in doing so would antagonize a sizable minority of her people. There would be ill will between Jumping Bull's relatives and hers. Some of Jumping Bull's friends might even seek vengeance on Nate. The whole village would be in an uproar for many moons with everyone taking sides, and if at all possible she wanted to avoid such a nightmare.

The day was pleasant, the air cool. Winona ran a hand through her long tresses and hummed as she walked. This was the first moment of true relaxation she had enjoyed in some time and she was in no rush to get back.

The first snare contained a rabbit. Winona hefted the animal a few times, judging how rigid the body had become, which in turn told her exactly how long it had been dead—in this case for at least one sleep. A few hours of boiling and she'd have a stew fit for a chief.

Loosening the cord around the rabbit's neck, Winona stuffed the rabbit into the parfleche and reset the hook snare. To do so she had to bend the sapling she had initially used down nearly to the ground, then lightly wedge the end of the sapling under the hooked branch she had previously pounded deep into the earth. The hook held the sapling in place until an unwary animal came along and stuck its head into the cord snare, which was attached to the sapling. The animal's struggles would then pull the sapling free of the hook and the slender tree would snap upright, sometimes breaking the animal's neck as it did. If not, the animal died from slow strangulation.

Winona patted the parfleche, picked up her lance, and moved on to the second snare. This one employed a cord greased thick with animal fat as bait on the stick that

David Thompson

served as the lever for the sapling. A loop was positioned inches from the greased cord so that the only way an animal could get at the grease was by sticking its head through the loop. Once it did, it triggered the stick and up whipped the sapling. Here she found a raccoon, its body still warm, which she stuffed into the parfleche on top of the rabbit.

After resetting the snare, Winona ambled off toward the third and last trap, situated at the base of a hill half a mile from the village. She daydreamed as she walked, thinking of the husband and son she loved so much and envisioning how happy she would be when they came back. She couldn't wait to hear about how Stalking Coyote shot his elk. She was positive he had, since Nate was an expert hunter and would guide the boy right to one.

Presently Winona came within sight of the third snare. She could tell from a distance that it had not been sprung, but she went close to make sure. Standing in a grassy clearing, she bent down and peered through the undergrowth until she distinguished the outline of the cord and the trigger. Both were untouched. Nodding, she began to rise when she heard rushing footsteps to her rear, and the next instant iron arms seized her from behind and she was lifted bodily into the air, then thrown down hard.

Winona hit on her left side. Stunned, she felt the lance being ripped from her grasp, the pistol being yanked from under her belt. Then a laugh that was more like a growl fell on her ears and gooseflesh erupted all over her body. Getting to one knee, she glanced up and snapped, "Jumping Bull!"

The warrior grinned triumphantly, turned, and hurled her weapons into a nearby thicket. "You won't be needing these," he commented.

"I thought you went hunting," Winona said, rising slowly, careful to keep her right hand on the hilt of her knife. She had to stall, to keep him talking until she

150

recovered. Then she would do what she had to, what she had already made up her mind she would do if this ever happened. It would be better if Jumping Bull's friends and family were incensed at *her*, not Nate. After all, they would hardly dare seek vengeance on a woman who had merely defended her honor.

Jumping Bull laughed and put his hands on his hips. A knife and a tomahawk adorned his waist and a quiver full of arrows rested on his back. Over his left shoulder was slung his bow. "I wanted you to think I had left with the others, when in truth I turned back once we reached the plain and circled around to where I could watch your lodge." His eyes roved over her from head to toe. "I've been watching and waiting for a long time, and now my patience has been rewarded."

"I do not see why you are so pleased with yourself," Winona said, backing up a stride so she would have room to swing her arm. "The men of our village will be furious with you once they hear you attacked me."

"You will never tell them."

"Why not?"

"Because I know women," Jumping Bull said. "I know the games you play with men, and how you say one thing when you really mean another."

"You think you know me?" Winona said coldly.

Jumping Bull lowered his arms and chuckled. "Once I have made you mine, you will not dare let anyone know what happened. You will pretend you are ashamed when really you are pleased that a man of your own people has taken you under his wing."

"And how will you make me yours?"

"How else?" Jumping Bull leered, and came toward her.

In a flash Winona's knife was out, the blade pointing at his stomach. "I will give you this one warning. Do not think to lay a hand on me or you will never live to

151

see your son grow to manhood."

Jumping Bull hesitated and stared at the gleaming blade. "You will not stab me," he declared. "In your heart you want me as much as I want you."

"I would sooner mate with a skunk."

"We shall see," Jumping Bull said confidently. Suddenly he lunged, grabbing at her wrist, but she was quicker, the knife licking out and slicing across his left palm. Drawing back, he held his hand up and blurted out, "You have drawn blood!"

"And I intend to draw a lot more unless you give me your word that you will leave me alone and not cause trouble for my husband when he comes back," Winona said, her legs coiled to spring or dodge depending on his next move. She was giving him this one final chance out of a innate reluctance to take the life of one of her own people. Since childhood she had been raised to regard the killing of another Shoshone as the supreme taboo, and she would violate it only as a last resort.

"How dare you!" Jumping Bull roared, and raising his other hand, he advanced to strike her. Again the knife flicked toward him, forcing him to pull away or be slashed open.

"What is wrong?" Winona taunted. "Is the great Jumping Bull afraid of one woman? What about all the coup you have counted? Were they on children?"

The warrior's face flushed bright scarlet. In his rage he sputtered, choking on the words he wanted to scream at her. Then, uttering a bestial snarl, he sprang.

Winona was prepared. She shifted and drove the point of the blade at his stomach. Jumping Bull jerked aside but the knife nicked him, tearing his buckskin shirt and pricking his flesh. Further incensed, he aimed a fist at her head, which missed when Winona skipped away. She circled again, crouching low, the flinty narrowing of her eyes showing that she was going for the kill. All her inhibitions had been stripped away in the heat of the moment. To preserve her family she was going to slay him or die in the attempt.

Jumping Bull, glowering fiercely, started to close with her, but the look on her face drew him up short. His glower vanished, to be replaced by astonishment. "You want to kill me!" he exclaimed.

"Yes!" Winona practically shouted, waving the knife. "So attack me! Come on! Do it! I want you dead so you will never bother me or my loved ones again."

A twisted smirk was Jumping Bull's reaction. "So that is it. You do this to save your man from my lance." He laughed harshly. "A nice attempt, woman, but I am no fool. I will not attack you." So saying, he calmly folded his arms across his chest and jutted his chin into the air. "But if you want to kill me, go ahead. I will not resist."

Winona swung her knife on high and advanced to strike, yet at the very moment she should have plunged the blade into her tormentor, she froze, chilled by the realization of the deed she was about to commit: outright murder.

"What is wrong?" Jumping Bull mocked her, using the same tone she had when mocking him. "Where is your courage? Can it be you will not kill someone who is defenseless?"

In desperation Winona took another half step and elevated the knife higher. For an instant their eyes locked, and to her horror she felt her resolve fading, her limbs weakening. But she must do it! she told herself. She must! She must!

The question was: Could she?

Chapter Twelve

Zach King was out of breath by the time he crawled to the top of the low hill, not from the exertion required but from the tingling excitement that rippled through his entire body, excitement so overwhelmingly intense he feared he might pass out. He paused, took a breath, and licked his lips, then glanced over his shoulder at the base of the hill where Mary and the pup stood. Over the past several days he had taught the little wolf to stay, and most of the time it obeyed reasonably well. Now, more than ever, it must do as he wanted, since any noise made might forewarn their enemies.

Holding the rifle close to his chest, Zach resumed his ascent. At the top a bush afforded enough shelter for him to rise to his knees. Carefully parting the thin branches, he gazed at the meadow below and nearly cried out in his consternation.

There were four Indians in sight, two of whom were busy gathering wood, a large pile of which already had been collected and placed on a spot between two adjacent cottonwoods. The other two were engaged in the act of tying his pa to those same trees, only they were tying him upside down so that his head hung a few feet above the growing stack of branches.

Zach's excitement gave way to unbridled fear. He knew enough of Indian ways to know they were going to burn his pa alive, a grisly form of torture made worse by the great suffering the victim endured since the flames were not permitted to engulf the unfortunate at once, but instead would burn slowly and thereby heighten the anguish.

From Zach's perch he could tell his pa was bad off. Blood caked his father's face and there were many welts and bruises. Worse, his pa hung limply, making no attempt to resist as the pair of warriors lashed him tight to the trees with stout cords. Tears welled up in Zach's eyes and he fought them back. His pa would soon die unless he did something.

But what? Zach wondered. He stood no chance against four grown men who would not think twice about slaying him on sight. Suddenly Zach stiffened, the thought forgotten. During the days spent on the trail he had figured out there were five warriors in the band, no difficult feat since two of the animals, evidently the two mules he saw tethered with the horses near the camp, had left shallower hoofprints, indicating those two had not borne the weight of riders. So his guess had proven right, but *where was the fifth warrior?*

Zach scanned the meadow and the surrounding forest. The last one must be in the woods somewhere, he figured, and he dared not make his move until the man reappeared. He didn't want to be taken by surprise at a crucial moment.

From the style of the shirts, leggins, and moccasins the Indians wore, Zach knew they weren't Blackfeet as he'd initially suspected. From the direction they were taking to go home, they might be Bloods, Piegans, or even Gros Ventres. It mattered little, since all of them had vowed to drive the whites from the mountains.

The pile of wood was growing apace. Soon the fire would be started. The warriors were talking and laughing as they worked. Every so often one of them, a lean, hawkish man, would walk up to their prisoner and strike him in a fit of sheer savagery.

Zach watched and went all cold inside. The time had come. His pa might already be close to death, so he dared not wait until the fifth Indian came back. Easing back from the bush, he angled to the left, working his way down the hill until he was in a thicket. From there he glided toward the camp, placing his feet down slowly and with his toes pointed inward as he had been taught so he made no noise. He stepped over twigs, avoided brush that might snag his clothes.

Soon Zach was close to where the horses and mules were tied. Beyond was the camp fire, and beyond that the pair of saplings from which his pa hung. He was close enough now to see a rivulet of blood flowing from his pa's mouth. For the first time in his young life, Zach experienced an unquenchable impulse to kill.

Flattening, Zach inched toward the animals. They were facing the fire so they wouldn't know he was there until he was right among them. Hopefully, they wouldn't whinny in alarm. He came up behind a mule, rose cautiously into a crouch, and patted the mule lightly on the flank as he stepped to the rope and drew his knife. Next to him a horse shifted and turned its head to eye him quizzically. Perhaps the fact he was a child allayed any fears the animal harbored, because it shortly looked away and ignored him.

Zach moved down the line, cutting each horse loose, keeping his eyes on the Indians in case one should face his way. None of them, though, were paying the least bit of attention to the animals; they were all too busy preparing the fire. At the end of the rope Zach ducked low and went around the last horse into tall grass.

Once under cover, Zach moved swiftly around behind the animals and past them into the sheltering forest. Rising on the shaded side of a towering pine, he cast about for a suitable stone, picked it up, and began to chuck it. Then his nerve faltered. What if something went wrong? he thought, and he actually trembled. The same old nagging objection presented itself, the thought that he was just a boy about to fight skilled warriors and he didn't stand a prayer.

Then Zach stared at his pa, the man he so dearly loved, the man who would do anything for him, who had saved his life more times than he cared to count. Could he do less in return? Gripping the stone firmly, he checked once to be sure the fifth warrior had not shown up yet, picked the nearest mule as the best target, and hurled the stone with all his might while at the selfsame instant he vented a screech like those he had heard panthers make.

Braying wildly, the mule executed a vertical leap, its back bent, its legs as stiff as boards. As it came down it crashed into the other mule, which in turn was knocked against a horse, and a moment later every last animal was in fearful flight across the meadow, the fleet horses in the lead.

Zach was also moving. He remembered what his pa had once said about fighting against superior odds: "Never stay in one place too long, son, or they'll pin you down and kill you at their convenience. Keep on the go and you can keep them off guard." So, bent at the waist, he dashed northward until he was about even with the cottonwoods but still 15 yards from them.

A large log offered Zach a place to hide. On his hands and knees, he lifted his head to see what the Indians were doing. Two of them were in hot pursuit of the animals, but the other two were advancing with weapons at the ready toward the spot where he had just been. By their tread and their attitude they were apparently uncertain as to the cause of the screech.

Zach waited until the two were out of sight before taking the next bold step. Without hesitation, he slid over the log and sprinted toward his unconscious father. He stayed low, watching the pair across the meadow enter the trees after the horses and mules. In moments he was at the pile of limbs. Crouching, he reached up and tenderly touched his father's severely bruised cheek. "Pa? It's me, Zach."

There was no response.

"Pa?" Zach persisted urgently, inadvertently raising his voice. "Can you hear me? You have to wake up?" He shook his father's shoulder. "Please, Pa!"

A few seconds went by. Nate's eyelids fluttered, and he became dimly aware of being upside down and in the most exquisite pain he had ever known. He also glimpsed his son, as if through a dense fog. "Zach?" he mumbled. "Is that you, son?"

"Yep," Zach answered, his throat so constricted he could barely talk. "We have to get you out of here, Pa. Those men will be back in a bit. Do you understand?"

"Do what you have to," Nate mumbled.

"Get set for a fall," Zach cautioned, applying his knife to the cords. "You're too heavy for me to hold up." He cut rapidly, the razor edge parting loop after loop. First he did the wrists. Then, resting the Kentucky rifle on the stacked branches, he quickly shimmied up the left-hand cottonwood until he was high enough to sever the cord binding his father's ankle. The instant he did, his father dropped, banging against the right-hand tree, still held

158

fast by the cord around the other ankle.

In the forest someone began shouting.

Zach's scalp prickled as he scrambled down, stepped to the other tree, and worked his way up to where he could get at the last cords. Feverishly, he sawed through them, and tried to grab hold of his father's leg to keep his pa from falling too hard. In this he only partially succeeded.

The shock of hitting the ground revived Nate again. He found himself on his back, staring up into a tree where his son clung to the slim trunk. "This isn't the time to be playing around," he chided, and tried to stand but couldn't. His legs were like mush, his mind not much better.

Zach let go and dropped. "Let me help, Pa," he said, looping an arm around his father's waist. The strain was tremendous and his knees nearly buckled, but somehow he got his father upright. "Hold steady now," he advised, and released his hold long enough to grab the rifle. "All right. Here we go."

To Nate they seemed to be walking in slow motion, even slower than his brain was working. He had difficulty recalling where he was or what was happening. Gradually, the more he moved, the more his circulation was restored, the more of his capture and subsequent torture he relived in his mind. He spied a log ahead. Abruptly, with startling vividness, he realized the grave risk his son was taking and his heart swelled with pride. "Where are the Gros Ventres?" he asked softly.

"Two of them are after their horses," Zach whispered. "Two more are in the trees yonder. I don't rightly know where the fifth one got to."

"You shouldn't have done this. You could be killed."

"If you don't go home, I don't go home."

"Zach—"

"Don't talk now, Pa. They might hear you."

Nate was too weak to protest. He did his best to walk under his own power, but his long-unused legs refused to cooperate. Gritting his teeth against the pain, he turned and checked the meadow and the line of trees to his left. "No Gros Ventres yet," he mumbled.

Zach prudently skirted the log, knowing his father was incapable of climbing over it. He breathed a hair easier when they were under cover, but he never slackened his pace. The Gros Ventres would return to the cotton-woods at any moment, and when they found their captive gone they would fly into a rage. If they were competent trackers, and most warriors were to some degree, they'd immediately give chase.

Suddenly Zach remembered the telltale spoor he must have left between the pine tree and the log. He'd tried to walk lightly, but everyone, no matter how good they were, made tiny smudges or bent grass or weeds as they went by. It surprised him that the two Gros Ventres who had gone into the forest hadn't found his trail yet.

The train of thought prompted Zach to look back, and it was well he did, for stealthily closing in were the warriors in question, the tall one in the lead grinning as if he was playing some grand game. The pair were less than ten feet away; they could have slain Zach and his father at any time. That they hadn't told Zach they wanted him and his pa alive.

"They're on us!" Zach shouted, slipping his left arm free and spinning. He brought the rifle up as he completed the turn. The tall warrior, still grinning, leaped, his arms outstretched, making no attempt to employ his lance. For a heartbeat Zach felt fear tug at his innards, and then he had the hammer pulled back and his finger was squeezing the trigger even though he didn't have the stock braced against his shoulder as he should.

160

The Kentucky boomed. A cloud of smoke enveloped the warrior's face. Zach was knocked backwards. He stumbled, and fell to one knee. Reversing his grip on the rifle, he held it like a club, ready to rain blows on the tall Gros Ventre. But there was no need. The warrior lay on his stomach, his head cocked to one side, his eyes locked wide in amazement, a gaping hole in the middle of his forehead.

Through the smoke rushed the second warrior, his features contorted in hatred. It was Bobcat, and his fury at having witnessed Rolling Thunder's death was boundless. Whatever their differences, they had been friends, had hunted and fought together for many years. Now he would avenge the loss. He blocked the awkward swing of the heavy rifle, grasped the barrel, and wrenched the gun loose. "Puny mosquito!" he rasped, throwing the gun down. "I will peel your skin off piece by piece!"

Zach didn't understand a word of the Gros Ventre tongue, but the meaning was clear. Drawing his knife, he slashed at the warrior's leg and missed. In trying to dart to one side, he misjudged his enemy's speed, and had his knife arm seized in an unbreakable grasp. He tried to pull loose, but was jerked off his feet and dangled in the air like a helpless minnow. His knife was torn from him and allowed to fall.

"You are brave, child," Bobcat declared. He glanced at Nate, who had collapsed and was doubled over. "If you were not white I would take you into my lodge and raise you as my own." Scowling, he shook Zach violently. "But you *are* white. You are an insect to be ground underfoot."

Zach had his teeth clenched to keep them from crunching together as he was shaken. He struggled uselessly to tear his arm free, then kicked at the warrior's groin. Much to his surprise, his foot connected, the Gros Ventre gurgled and turned scarlet, and he was unceremoniously dumped onto the ground.

"You die, boy!" Bobcat screamed, a hand over his privates. "Sing your death song!" Hissing, he drew his knife and pounced.

Lying flat on his back, Zach was helpless. He brought up his hands to try to ward off the blade and cast his final-ever glance at his father, but his father wasn't there. The next second he heard a thud and a grunt, and he looked up in bewilderment to behold a knife hilt jutting from the side of the warrior's neck. Then, over the Gros Ventre's shoulder, he saw his pa.

So intent had Bobcat been on the young one, he hadn't seen Grizzly Killer pick up the boy's discarded knife and rise. The first intimation he had of danger was the searing pain of the blade's penetration. He reached up, touched the hilt, realized what had occurred, and ignoring the pain, whirled to plunge his own knife into Grizzly Killer. Unexpectedly, his ankles were seized by slender arms. His momentum brought him down, and as he fell Grizzly Killer moved aside.

Bobcat saw the boy holding onto his legs and tried to kick the gnat off. He opened his mouth to vent his fury, but all that came out was blood. In a burst of temper, he seized the hilt of the knife in his neck, ripped it out, and leaned forward to plant both blades in the boy's back. He never completed the act. His head abruptly swam, his arms became leaden. He sagged, keeled over on his side, and felt his body convulsing. Stop it! he wanted to scream. I have whites to kill! Through a crimson haze he saw the boy stand, saw the father appear beside him. Vainly he endeavored to lunge at them, but a black veil enfolded him in its ebony clutches.

"He's dead, son," Nate said softly, leaning on Zach's shoulder for support. "Now get me out of here before the others show up."

Zach nodded mechanically, watching the growing puddle form under the slain Gros Ventre.

"Now," Nate reiterated.

As if awakening from a deep sleep, Zach stirred to life and nodded. He reclaimed his knife, shoved it in its sheath, then gave the other knife to his father, who also took the lance and tomahawk belonging to the tall warrior. Zach scooped up his rifle.

"This way, Pa. We have to go south now."

They hurried as best they were able, managing no better than a rapid walk, the boy lending a hand when the father's exhaustion gained the upper hand. Zach expected to see the remaining warriors come racing through the brush at any moment, and he wanted to stop so he could reload the rifle. Every delay, however, increased the odds of being overtaken. They must press on and hope they reached the mare before the Gros Ventres showed.

In a short while the hill reared before them, and Zach led his father to the left along its base. They bypassed the thicket since Zach wasn't sure his father could make it through, and as they stepped into the open a hair-raising shriek pierced the air.

Loud Talker was the one who uttered it as he took several long strides and swooped down from the slope above them like an oversized bird of prey. His powerful body rammed into Grizzly Killer's chest, clipping the boy in the bargain, and all three of them went down in a whirl of arms and legs and weapons.

The first on his feet, Loud Talker dove at Grizzly Killer. He rated the father as the deadlier foe, the one to be dispatched first. In so doing, he neglected to take into account the compelling power of the love of a child for its parent. His right hand was on Grizzly Killer's throat, his left sweeping the tomahawk high for a lethal stroke, when excruciating, burning pain exploded in his lower back and spiked the length of his spine.

Loud Talker pivoted on his left heel, or tried to, but was thwarted when his legs went numb. Stupefied, he spied the boy a few feet off holding a dripping knife. "You!" he blurted, whipping the tomahawk back to throw it. Again was he frustrated when his arms also went numb. Then his neck. And his face. The boy speared the knife at his chest, but all Loud Talker could do was gape in dumb disbelief. He felt nothing, no pain, no blood on his skin, absolutely nothing until an icy mist gushed from within the core of his being and bore him into an abysmal chasm.

Breathlessly, Zach leaped clear as the warrior toppled. He dashed to his rising father and wordlessly offered his body as a living crutch. Together they hastened toward Mary, visible through the trees.

Suddenly the fourth Gros Ventre was upon them. Walking Bear had been sprinting over the top of the hill when Loud Talker was struck low, and with his lips set in a grim line he bore down on the shuffling white and the slight breed. Slaughter was in his heart, fire in his glare, a lance poised in his right hand. He knew they heard him, saw them swing around, and threw his lance.

Had it not been for the tomahawk Nate held in his left hand, his life would have ended right then and there. The lance struck the flat head of the tomahawk, smashing the weapon against his chest and stunning him. But the head deflected the tip of the lance enough to send it sailing over his shoulder.

Walking Bear never broke stride. In a trice he was on the boy, a corded arm clubbing him to the ground before the knife could be employed. Like a striking snake his hand lashed out, closing on the boy's throat. Gleefully, Walking Bear hoisted the squirming Zach into the air and squeezed.

At that juncture a new element was added to the fray, a flash of fur and teeth that clamped onto Walking Bear's right leg, razor teeth buried to the bone.

Agony coursed up Walking Bear's thigh and he looked down, dumfounded to discover a feral wolf pup trying to chew his limb completely through. Instinctively he snapped his leg, yet the wolf proved persistent, clinging to him like glue. Infuriated, he flung the boy to the earth and grabbed for the wolf, never seeing the weaving specter that drove the glittering point of a lance clean through his skull.

Zach shoved to his feet as his father fell. "Pa!" he exclaimed, at Nate's side in two bounds. "Pa?"

The effort had nearly depleted Nate's meager reservoir of strength. He smiled wanly and rose onto his elbows. "I can make it to the mare," he said. "But I'll need a hand."

"Anything."

Nate bunched his shoulders, started to rise. A bundle of sinew and hair materialized under his face and commenced licking him energetically. "Call this brute off," he joked. "I don't care to be eaten alive."

Clasping the pup under one arm, his other about his father, Zach steered them toward Mary. Repeatedly he scanned the hill and glanced over his shoulder. There was still the fifth warrior to deal with, the one who had been missing earlier. The man was bound to have heard the noise. So where was he?

The mare shied as they approached, frightened by the tangy scent of moist blood. She bobbed her head, the reins flying, and pranced a dozen yards from the hill.

"Remind me to shoot her when we get back," Nate muttered, slumping to his knees. "You fetch her, son. I couldn't catch a turtle."

Zach dutifully complied, setting Blaze down so he could grab the reins when Mary let him get close enough.

Anxious minutes were spent chasing her before she finally did, and he was tempted to cuff her until he recalled his father saying that any man who mistreated an animal was an animal himself. Yanking hard to let her know who was boss, he led her back.

If ever a man appeared to have a foot at death's door, it was Nate. His breath was ragged, his chest heaving. Blanching, he fanned his stamina, and managed to stand and grip the saddle. Without his son's assistance he wouldn't have been able to mount, and once astride Mary he had to hold on with both hands for fear of falling.

Zach climbed up in front of his father, adjusted the rifle on his hips, and remarked, "Hold on to me, Pa. I'll get you home. I promise."

Blaze yipped, Mary snorted, and they were off, heading south, making for the mountains. Zach constantly shifted to check to their rear.

"What's wrong?" Nate asked.

"The fifth warrior, Pa. Where did he go?"

"Hunting, I think."

"He must have gone far."

"Far enough. Be thankful he didn't make it back. We never would have gotten out of there."

A solitary figure standing on the south slope of the hill amidst a cluster of trees slowly lowered the bow he had taken from Bobcat's corpse and relaxed his fingers. The arrow he had ready to fly slipped from the string. He stared at Loud Talker, then at Walking Bear, and out at the retreating riders and their frisky friend. "I knew," he said softly.

Turning, the figure wended his lonely way up and over the hill, and paused to somberly regard the pile of branches between the cottonwoods. "I knew," he repeated. "Why wouldn't he listen?"

Slinging the bow over his shoulder, he hiked to the bottom of the hill and made one more pertinent comment: "It is for the best. White Buffalo will make a better chief than *he* ever could have been."

Epilogue

The women were out gathering roots to the northwest of the village when one of them saw the horse and called out. Since they never knew when enemies might conduct a raid, they were tensed to flee until Winona recognized the two people on the weary mare. Throwing her basket aside, she sped to meet them with joy on her face.

"Grizzly Killer! Stalking Coyote!" she cried, tears filling her eyes. So happy was she to see them safe and alive that she gave no thought to them both being on Mary. They alighted and came to her, arms flung wide.

Winona was nearly bowled over. Elated, she hugged them and smothered their cheeks with wet kisses. "I missed you!" she declared. "What took you so long?"

Neither of them uttered a word.

Drawing back, Winona noted their moist eyes. She also got a good look at her husband's face and recoiled, aghast. "What happened to you? Who did this?" Her gaze strayed to Mary. "And where is Pegasus?"

"Dead," Nate said simply.

"Gros Ventres," Zach added.

Intuition told Winona the extent of their ordeal, and she wisely refrained from badgering them with questions. They would, she knew, tell her later, when they were comfortably settled in the lodge. "Come. You must be hungry. I have rabbit stew simmering."

"Can Blaze have some too?" Zach asked, reverting to English since there was no word in Shoshone that corresponded to the name he had bestowed on the pup.

"Who?"

Zachary pointed toward the mare. The wolf lay close to Mary's front hoofs, chin on its paws, its tongue lolling. "Pa said it's all right for me to keep him."

"He did?" Winona said, recalling how Nate had vowed to never have another such pet after the death of their devoted dog. "Then I guess I have no objections so long as it stays outside as the rest of the dogs in the village do."

Nate coughed and said rather sheepishly, "It can sleep inside if it wants."

"Oh."

Keenly aware of her penetrating stare, Nate changed the subject by pointing at a tall tree to the west in which a large platform had been constructed high in the branches. "Did someone die while we were gone?"

"Yes," Winona said, walking to the horse and taking the reins. "I will bring Mary. You two can go on ahead and help yourself to the stew."

"Who was it, Ma?" Zach inquired. "Anyone we were close to?"

"No."

"Who then?"

The answer was a full five seconds in coming, and when it did her voice was level, composed. The faintest of smiles touched the corners of her mouth as she responded, "Jumping Bull."

WILDERNESS

Fang & Claw
David Thompson

To survive in the untamed wilderness a man needs all the friends he can get. No one can battle the continual dangers on his own. Even a fearless frontiersman like Nate King needs help now and then and he's always ready to give it when it's needed. So when an elderly Shoshone warrior comes to Nate asking for help, Nate agrees to lend a hand. The old warrior knows he doesn't have long to live and he wants to die in the remote canyon where his true love was killed many years before, slain by a giant bear straight out of Shoshone myth. No Shoshone will dare accompany the old warrior, so he and Nate will brave the dreaded canyon alone. And as Nate soon learns the hard way, some legends are far better left undisturbed.

___4862-0 $3.99 US/$4.99 CAN

Dorchester Publishing Co., Inc.
P.O. Box 6640
Wayne, PA 19087-8640

THE BIG FIFTY

JOHNNY D. BOGGS

Young Coady McIlvain spends his days reading about the heroic exploits of the legendary heroes of the West, especially the glorious Buffalo Bill Cody. The harsh reality of frontier life in Kansas becomes brutally clear to Coady, however, when his father is scalped and he is taken prisoner by Comanches. When he is finally able to escape, Coady finds himself with a buffalo sharpshooter who he imagines is the living embodiment of his hero, Buffalo Bill. But real life is seldom like a dime novel, and Fate has more hard lessons in store for Coady—if he can stay alive to learn them.

PETER DAWSON

GHOST BRAND OF THE WISHBONES

Peter Dawson's fiction has retained its classic status among readers of many generations. This volume presents for the first time in paperback three of his most enduring short novels. The title tale opens with the daring robbery of an entire cattle train and gets only more exciting from there. "Hell's Half Acre" is filled with the chaos and danger that results from an all-out range war between cattle ranchers and the sheep raising syndicate. And in "Sagerock Sheriff," old Tom Platt faces his toughest challenge since he took office years ago. He has to find out—right away—if a man being sentenced to life in the penitentiary is really guilty of murder.

Dorchester Publishing Co., Inc.
P.O. Box 6640
Wayne, PA 19087-8640

_____5320-9
$4.99 US/$6.99 CAN

Name: _____

Address: _____

City: _____ State: _____ Zip: _____

E-mail: _____

I have enclosed $_____ in payment for the checked book(s).

For more information on these books, check out our website at www.dorchesterpub.com.
_____ _Please send me a free catalog._